"Kiss her!"

Someone in the crowd had called out the suggestion, but Olivia wasn't about to let that happen. "Hey, knock it off." She tried to wiggle out of Luke's grasp.

He didn't let go.

Olivia glanced at him in surprise. Uh-oh, she knew that look. *What a wonderful idea,* it said. "You don't have to kiss me."

"I want to." His thumbs began a meticulous inventory of her ribs, causing sensations somewhere between a tickle and—

No! Kissing him would be a monumental mistake. "It isn't necessary. Really."

"I'm going to." He moved closer, smiling wickedly.

Olivia's heart pounded. Oh, well, everyone was entitled to a mistake or two. "If you insist. But remember, it won't be a real kiss."

"Yes, it will."

And it was.

Dear Reader,

"Howdy, y'all. Welcome to Texas!" The speaker was a Texas Ranger. My family was driving to our new home in Houston and had just crossed the Texas-Oklahoma border where we'd stopped at the welcome station operated by the highway department. After the ranger greeted us, he handed my brother, sister and me a package of bluebonnet seeds, the state flower of Texas. Lady Bird Johnson's Beautify America campaign, which spread wildflowers along the nation's highways, had started a few years earlier. The ranger instructed us to "throw the seeds out the window somewhere between here and Houston."

As my parents studied maps, my sister, a toddler, chewed on her packet of seeds. My brother ran outside and promptly dumped his seeds on the asphalt parking lot. We got back in the car only to stop at the next roadside park so my sister could wash bluebonnet seeds out of her mouth. We made her spit them in the grass, so perhaps they actually grew.

I wanted to save my seeds and plant them at our new house. But a *Texas Ranger,* in uniform, had told me I should throw them out the window. I compromised by releasing one tiny bluebonnet seed every ten miles for the next three hundred miles and planted the few remaining seeds in our front yard.

Other Texas travelers must have done a better job planting seeds, because April in Texas is spectacular. Waves of blue, splashed with orange and yellow, line the highways. Bluebonnet Ranch in *Counterfeit Cowgirl* is set right in the middle of the beautiful Hill Country—and it *is* beautiful. But don't just take my word for it—y'all come on down.

Sincerely,

Heather Allison

COUNTERFEIT COWGIRL

Heather Allison

Harlequin Books

TORONTO • NEW YORK • LONDON
AMSTERDAM • PARIS • SYDNEY • HAMBURG
STOCKHOLM • ATHENS • TOKYO • MILAN
MADRID • WARSAW • BUDAPEST • AUCKLAND

To Mary Elizabeth Hickman Barger
with gratitude for her work on the family history.

Special thanks to Pat Kay, Alaina Richardson,
Carla Luan, Marilyn Amann and Sue Royer
for their genuinely good critiques.

ISBN 0-373-03309-5

COUNTERFEIT COWGIRL

This edition published by arrangement with Harlequin Enterprises B. V.

Printed in U.S.A.

CHAPTER ONE

"FIRED? THE WHOLE writing staff?" Olivia Faraday raised one eyebrow. The unmade-up one. So that's what was behind this morning's summons of the entire *Lovers and Liars* cast.

"Yes," moaned the petite blonde behind her. She paced across Olivia's dressing room twice, then flopped onto the flowered couch.

"Is this your first purge?" Olivia regarded her pouting colleague in the mirror above the vanity.

"You mean you've been through this before?" Monique, the blonde, sighed heavily.

"Several times." Olivia considered her reflection, specifically her eyebrows. She covered the thinner, lighter one with her hand, then covered the heavier darker one for comparison.

"Aren't you worried at all?" Monique's face was the perfect picture of worry.

Olivia wasn't worried—yet. More mildly concerned, and only because it was unusual to fire *all* the writing staff at once.

Besides, worrying caused wrinkles, and Olivia was at the stage of her career when she was more concerned about the wrinkles on her face than wrinkles in the writing staff. But Monique wasn't as experienced and obviously looked to Olivia for reassurance. "Sometimes a wholesale cleaning can be good," she offered.

Monique jumped up and began pacing again. "They just let me age a little." Olivia rolled her eyes. "The new team will probably have me back doing teen story lines. I'm twenty-four! How long do they think I can pass for seventeen?"

About as long as they expected Olivia to pass for twenty-four. She hoped her thirtieth birthday had sneaked by unnoticed.

"*You* won't have any problems. They won't mess with Diana D'Angelo."

"They'd better not." Olivia had spent twelve years developing Diana D'Angelo from a secondary character into the most popular female character on the New York-based soap opera *Lovers and Liars.* In fact, Diana was one of the most popular characters on *any* soap opera, and Olivia worked hard to keep her that way.

With a groan, Monique flung herself back onto the couch. "Do you think the slip in the ratings had anything to do with the writers being fired?"

Did the slip have any... Slowly Olivia swiveled to face Monique. "Monique, *dahling,*" she said in her best Diana voice. "Even the bubbleheaded twit you play could figure that out."

But Monique was too upset to smile. "Do you think I *like* playing a bubbleheaded twit?"

"Sorry, I was only—"

"Do you think I *like* wearing tight T-shirts and knowing I'll spend each summer parading around in a swimsuit so we can attract the preadolescent males who are home from school and are too young to work at the local Burger Doodle?" Amazingly Monique didn't run out of breath. Olivia was impressed. That girl had had some serious vocal coaching.

"Okay, you're too good for the Noelle part." Olivia swiveled back. "A piece of advice. Endure. Do what it takes to last in this business."

"Why? They don't give Emmys for endurance."

"Sure they do. All the time."

"*You* don't have an Emmy."

In the mirror, Olivia's level gaze met Monique's slightly malicious one. "No, but I do have my self-respect."

Pink stained Monique's face. Moments later, she groaned again. "I hate this waiting!"

"Here." Olivia tossed her an eyebrow pencil. "Do your eyebrows."

"I've been meaning to ask you—what's with the eyebrows?" Monique pulled a hassock up to the mirror and sat. Her chin barely cleared the vanity top.

Olivia shoved jars and tubes aside until she uncovered a gold-colored memo. She dangled it in front of Monique.

Monique squinted. "'To: All female actresses. From: Wardrobe and Makeup. Subject: Eyebrows.' *I* didn't get one of these. Nobody ever tells me anything."

"You don't do your own makeup."

"Oh." She continued, "'In order for *Lovers and Liars* to maintain the fashionable image our viewers have come to expect...' Blah blah—here it is, '...this season, eyebrows will be thicker to reflect the current direction in fashion.'" She stopped and stared at Olivia, who obligingly covered first one eye, then the other. "Oh, no."

"That's what I thought," Olivia said, reaching for the cleansing cream. "Besides, I thought eyebrows were going thinner."

"Ha. I like the addendum. 'Actresses will refrain from adding shoulder pads to clothing. Large shoulder pads are no longer fashion forward.' Shows how little they know. Shoulder pads would look really fashion forward on a strapless two-piece." Monique sounded so disgusted that Olivia laughed. After a moment, Monique did, too.

"We'll just pretend we never saw this." Olivia plucked the paper out of Monique's hands and deliberately tore it into two. Then she dropped the pieces into the trash can. "Things will be so unsettled for the next few days that our eyebrows will be the least of their worries."

But not the least of *her* worries. Although for Monique's sake—and maybe her own—Olivia wanted to appear only mildly concerned about the inconvenience of breaking in a new writing team, this shake-up was beginning to feel different from any of the others.

The ratings slip had been at first a slide, then a complete free-fall. It was a fact that whenever Olivia took time off, which wasn't often, the show's popularity dipped. Olivia made sure she took time off right before her contract was up for renewal. Producers had a tendency to take her for granted.

But this time, the ratings hadn't climbed when Diana D'Angelo came back. Diana was between story lines, which was another reason Olivia had taken her vacation. When she returned, there was no new, glamorous story line, no new, glamorous wardrobe and no new, handsome leading man. Most male characters on "Lovers and Liars" were introduced as Diana's new lover, since Diana had been involved with all the current male leads.

No new story line, and see what had happened? No ratings climb.

Olivia did not feel vindicated. Why hadn't there been a new story line for her? Something wasn't right. What an awful time for negotiating a contract.

The sharp knock on the door made both women jump. "You're wanted in the conference room," said a voice, then footsteps moved down the hall and the message was repeated.

Monique sat frozen.

"It'll be okay," Olivia reassured her. "They won't make horrendous changes right away. It's just not done."

Monique didn't thaw.

"Hey." Olivia jostled her arm. "We're talking about people who send out memos on eyebrows."

Monique managed a weak and unconvincing smile.

The rest of the cast emerged from their dressing rooms where they'd spent most of the morning and afternoon waiting for news. No one spoke as they shuffled down the hall to the elevators. Once inside, everyone concentrated on the floor numbers. Their nervousness began to rub off on Olivia.

A collection of attractive people wearing unattractive frowns, they filed into the staff conference room. From the litter of coffee cups, sandwich wrappers and cigarette stubs, Olivia gathered that the new writers had been brainstorming all night.

John Paul, the producer, clapped his hands for attention. "People, I'd like you to meet your new writers. They've worked like crazy to come up with an innovative bible and next week's scripts. I'll distribute copies as soon as my girl gets back."

Babble broke out immediately at the news that there was to be a different bible—stories outlined for the next several years. The writers wore tight smiles and refused to meet anyone's eyes.

"I'd also like you to meet our new sponsor, Collingsworth Industries."

Olivia hadn't noticed the jowly, gray-haired man in the corner. He seemed to disapprove of everyone and everything.

Olivia wasn't surprised that *Lovers and Liars* had a new advertiser. When ratings fell, so did the cost of advertising time. Collingsworth Industries had gone bargain hunting.

Just then John Paul's "girl" returned with a stack of script copies, and the actors pounced on them.

"Olivia?"

She looked at John Paul.

"We'd like to talk with you after the others leave."

Olivia's heart stopped, then began racing. She didn't like the sound of this.

The room resonated with ominous quiet after her fellow cast members left. John Paul introduced her to the Collingsworth Industries representative, who turned out to be Mr. Collingsworth himself.

This was unusual. Olivia wanted to wipe her hand before shaking his so he wouldn't be able to tell how nervous she was. However, Mr. Collingsworth remained seated and didn't look as though he'd shake her hand even if she offered it. Olivia immediately characterized him as a very conservative, traditional man of her father's generation, who wasn't quite ready to accept the acquaintance of an actress.

"Ah, Olivia," began John Paul, slowly handing her the bible. "We're going to be taking the show in a fresh direction..."

This didn't sound good, Olivia thought as she accepted the sheaf of papers.

"And I, for one, am excited about it." John Paul shook his fist as he said the word "excited."

Since John Paul was only excited when it behooved him to be, that meant the changes were dictated by the sponsor, who must have put up major bucks. Olivia glanced at Collingsworth with renewed interest.

"Have a seat." John Paul gestured to the one he'd occupied. "And take a few minutes to familiarize yourself with Diana's new story line."

Olivia sat. The changes must be horrendous if John Paul thought she couldn't read them standing up.

As she flipped through the bible, Olivia was aware that the writers skulked from the room, but that Mr. Collingsworth remained. Oh, joy.

John Paul was silent, watching her.

Olivia quickly glanced at the casting, then read it again, more slowly. It was a bloodbath. *What* were they doing? At least a third of the characters were either being written out or recast. Hers wasn't one of them. In spite of her relief, she very much resented feeling that her replacement might have been a possibility.

She noted that Monique's character, Noelle, was still there, but shipwrecked on a spring-break cruise. Poor Monique. That meant even more time in torn clothes and bathing suits.

But what was up with Diana? Olivia scanned until she found the outline for her story.

"A *ranch*?" Olivia read with disbelief. "Diana D'Angelo inherits a ranch? In the West?" She glared at John Paul. "How nice."

"Yes, isn't it?" His smile was as fake as his hair.

There was more. "On-location shoots," Olivia warbled. "Why, John Paul, what will this do to production costs?" *Are you crazy?* her expression said.

Humor the sponsor, dear, his look replied. "Did you hear that, Mr. Collingsworth? Is she a team player, or what?"

Mr. Collingsworth grunted suspiciously.

"'Diana, in an effort to learn more about her inheritance, works as a *ranch hand,*'" Olivia emphasized, with a glance at John Paul. "And I see she'll have a new wardrobe. Jeans, flannel shirts..." This was insane.

"You know..." Olivia bit her lip and looked off into space as if a thought had only just occurred to her. "I can really see Diana inheriting the ranch. Frankly, she's needed another source of income to support the lifestyle the public seems to expect." Olivia smiled at Mr. Collingsworth. "You may not know this, but Diana is sort of a—" she gestured with her hands, deliberately drawing his attention to the perfectly manicured nails and the official Diana jewelry "—fantasy character. She's glamorous, wealthy—a bit spoiled, it's true—but endearing. She doesn't deal with small, mundane irritants. Other people deal with them for her. She leads the kind of life women dream about. They identify with her. When Diana wears beautiful clothes and eats in elegant restaurants and falls in love with handsome men who adore her, our viewers can experience those things too."

"She's been married too many times," Mr. Collingsworth said.

Olivia blinked. "Well, yes, I suppose six times is a bit above average. But Diana's life is so full, and she has so many more experiences than most—"

"And this will be just another one of those experiences, won't it, Olivia?" John Paul interrupted, taking the seat across from her.

"Yes, yes, of course." Not if she could help it. "I merely meant to suggest that Diana wouldn't actually have to *live* at the ranch, at least not on camera. Working as a ranch hand doesn't seem to be the sort of fantasy that fits the Diana character."

Mr. Collingsworth looked mulish. John Paul registered this and sent Olivia a pleading glance.

Okay, she'd try another argument. "It would save money to allude to the ranch and perhaps tape Diana's return when she's dressed in Western chic. You know, turquoise and suede?" In Olivia's experience, the magic words were "save money."

"What's the matter with her?" Mr. Collingsworth asked John Paul.

John Paul cleared his throat. "She's concerned about pleasing the viewers, as we all are. Isn't that so, Olivia?"

"Oh, yes, very concerned."

"Honest work will do Diana good. Mrs. Collingsworth has been concerned about her moral character."

Groaning inwardly, Olivia scanned the rest of her story line, something she should have done before shooting off her mouth. What she read made her blood run cold. Not only was Diana inheriting a ranch, she was inheriting a previously unknown cousin, Megan Malloy. In fact, Diana was inheriting Megan's family ranch. Olivia skipped past the convoluted reasons Diana was the heir instead of Megan and searched for the conclusion of the story line.

The writers obviously hadn't had the time to come up with more than a few sketchy details, but what she read was bad enough. Someone was kicked in the head by a horse and lapsed into a coma.

"Excuse me," she said, interrupting the murmured conference between John Paul and Mr. Collingsworth. "Whose coma is this?"

John Paul dropped his gaze and Olivia held her breath.

"Well—" he shot a sidelong glance at Mr. Collingsworth and puffed out his cheeks "—we, uh, haven't really decided yet."

In other words, the ratings and the sponsor would decide. Olivia understood perfectly. If the public didn't like Megan, this was an easy way to get rid of her character. And if the public didn't like the new Diana...

She exhaled in a reverse gasp. A coma. Olivia had been in the business too long not to know the significance of a coma. It could mean recasting. Or death. And death of a major character would result in months of wonderful publicity.

This was a disaster. They might kill off Diana and replace her with a younger version. "Is it wise to invest so much time and effort in a story line when we haven't fully thought out the ending?" Olivia tried to sound thoughtful and concerned. A team player. If they'd give her a few minutes, she'd come up with an ending herself. Now, which of the new writers was responsible for her lines?

"Olivia, *darling,* I share your concern about *developing* this new *dimension* of Diana's character. But you'll grow as an actress. Think of the *demands* on your talent." John Paul was speaking in his humor-the-big-star voice.

"Oh, I am, I am." She smiled a big-star smile. "Convincing comas are such a challenge."

Mr. Collingsworth eyed John Paul with suspicion. The new sponsor was a good judge of character, Olivia noted.

John Paul's eyes narrowed. "Mr. Collingsworth, why don't we share our ideas on the ranch story with Diana—I mean, Olivia."

Olivia knew the slip on her name had been deliberate. Just a subtle reminder that she was being difficult.

She didn't care. So far, being cooperative had landed her a story line with a coma. Definitely a dead end, as far as character development.

"We'll be shooting on location at Bluebonnet Ranch in Texas," John Paul informed her. "You've heard of the Bluebonnet Foundation?"

"No," Olivia was forced to admit.

"We work with juvenile authorities and the schools to find inner-city youth we feel will benefit from a change in environment," recited Mr. Collingsworth. "I handle the New York end, and Luke handles the ranch end."

"Luke?" Olivia asked.

"Lucas Chance." Mr. Collingsworth handed her literature emblazoned with bluebonnets. "He started the program and owns the ranch where we send the kids. I want more people to know about it."

"And they will, they will." Impatiently John Paul turned to Olivia, who was unfolding the brochure. "It seems Mrs. Collingsworth is a fan of yours, Olivia."

"Is she?" Olivia beamed at Mr. Collingsworth.

He nodded. "Never misses a show."

"Really?" Olivia sent a triumphant look to John Paul. "Doesn't Mrs. Collingsworth sound like a lovely woman, John Paul?"

"Lovely. But I told the Collingsworths this would be quite a departure for you. And I know the coma presents a challenge to your acting abilities."

How dare he tease her like that! Olivia stretched her foot under the table and kicked him. "I'm always willing to grow as an actress."

John Paul gave a strained chuckle. "Mr. Collingsworth, Olivia and I need to talk through a few technicalities. Would you like my girl to give you a tour?"

Mr. Collingsworth didn't look as though he'd enjoy a tour, but within moments, John Paul and Olivia were ushering him out the door. They maintained their smiles until the door was firmly closed.

"You *kicked* me!" John Paul stalked over to the conference table and gathered the script copies.

"You bet I kicked you!" Olivia snatched her script back from him. "You made me look bad in front of the sponsor."

"And it wasn't difficult, since you kept griping about Diana's story line!"

"With good reason! Have you lost your mind? Women don't want to watch Diana commune with nature. They want to see her new wardrobe, her new lovers."

"It's getting difficult to find a man who hasn't already been Diana's lover," was John Paul's dry comment.

That was true and silenced Olivia momentarily.

"So, dear, you'll have a new wardrobe, a new lover, a new enemy and a new story line." He headed toward the door, stopping with his hand on the knob. "Why the complaints?"

"Because you're deliberately destroying Diana."

"Don't be absurd," he denied quickly.

"I'm not being absurd!" She tried another tack. "You see my hair?" She grabbed a hank and held it out. "Dark brown, slightly angled, parted on the left, currently one inch below my chin."

"Yes?"

"As specified in my contract," she emphasized. "I can't trim it more than half an inch without prior approval."

"Olivia, if you want a new hairstyle, we can negotiate."

She made a frustrated sound. "My point is that my image—Diana's image—is so regulated that I even have a public appearance clause. What I wear has to be something Diana might wear. That's how important Diana is to *Lovers and Liars*. She's practically a franchise. And they want to change her completely."

"Practically a franchise?" John Paul gave a crack of laughter and opened the door. "Contract-renewal time, is it? Don't you leave haggling to your agent?"

Reaching around John Paul, Olivia slammed the door and wedged her foot against it, preventing his escape. "All right, what's really going on?"

John Paul muttered, shoved his hands into his pockets and muttered some more. "It's the old golden rule," he said at last. "He who has the gold makes the rule."

"Mr. Collingsworth," guessed Olivia staring at the script in her hands. "So the network's willing to let him ruin *Lovers and Liars*?"

"Careful, careful." John Paul patted her on the cheek. "He believes he's injecting a dose of much-needed morality. And at the end of every episode, there'll be a public-service announcement telling viewers how to contact the Bluebonnet Foundation."

"How very noble."

"And all the production costs become a tax write-off."

"Now I see the appeal," she said cynically. "But I've spent twelve years creating Diana. I don't want to jeopardize her for a tax write-off."

John Paul's eyes glittered. "Either you cooperate, or Diana goes into a coma from which she'll never recover."

He'd carry through with his threat, too, but Olivia wasn't about to let him see he'd intimidated her. "Is there any way I can change your mind about this ranch thing?"

John Paul shook his head. "In fact, the set crew is flying there tomorrow. The ranch buildings need a face-lift. You'll join us at the end of the week."

"What?" Olivia stared at him.

John Paul wore a bland expression. "We need to film outdoor footage, and it's bluebonnet season in Texas. Very picturesque. Lucas Chance, the ranch owner, is on a tight schedule and insists we come immediately or not at all."

"Insists?" Olivia's voice rose. "Who does this Lucas Chance think he is?"

CHAPTER TWO

LUCAS CHANCE WAS A SAINT.

Selfless, gentle, kind, patient, generous to the point of bankruptcy, admired and adored by all.

At least according to awards and testimonials in the Bluebonnet brochures. Olivia had read them twice. Once during the plane ride and again during what was turning out to be a rather lengthy taxi ride. The cab-driver wasn't running the air-conditioning, so Olivia had endured an hour and a half of muggy April air blowing through the windows.

She'd landed in Austin, Texas, expecting to be met by either someone from *Lovers and Liars* or someone from Bluebonnet Ranch. When it became apparent that no one was meeting her, she did what any New Yorker would do—she hired a taxi.

She'd had no idea the ranch was so far from civilization. It was bluebonnet season and waves of them lined the two-lane blacktop road, along with neon-orange Indian paintbrush and delicate pink and yellow primroses. Though the wildflowers were spectacular, after riding west for miles with only the silent cab-driver, she'd begun to worry.

After all, she *was* Diana D'Angelo, although she was not currently dressed for the part. She'd had more than her share of encounters with fans who forgot that Diana was just a character portrayed by an actress with a very different personality.

What if she was being kidnapped? Here she was, out in the wilds of Texas—miles and miles of open land, scrubby bushes and an odd tree or two. Granted the hills were gorgeous. Not the tamed rolling hills of New York, but rough, unmolded gouges of land with creamy white boulders exposed like the bones of a carcass.

Carcass. Shivering, she asked the driver, "How much farther?"

Silently he pointed.

"Okay, just down the road." Her voice dripped with amiability. She didn't want him to feel threatened. "How many more miles down the road?"

"A couple."

Exactly what he'd said the last three times she'd asked. Great. A Texas mile was obviously much longer than a New York mile. There was no ranch around here. She'd seen *Dallas*. She knew what a ranch was supposed to look like.

And where were all the oil wells? Didn't Texas have a lot of oil wells?

They'd been driving for so long, maybe they weren't even in Texas anymore.

Just after she'd managed to thoroughly scare herself, the taxi slowed and turned onto an unmarked road. Even though she'd been watching for anything remotely indicating civilization, the unprepossessing entrance of Bluebonnet Ranch surprised her.

A white wooden sign embellished with a stem of Texas bluebonnets pointed down the packed dirt road to a cluster of buildings. Olivia compared the stark iron arch over the gate to the fresh white paint of the sign and detected the work of the set crew. This must be the place. She forced herself to take deep, calming breaths, coughing as dust swirled in through the windows.

The first thing she'd do when she was shown to her room was take a nice wet bath while sipping a nice dry Chardonnay.

But this was Texas, so maybe she'd have to settle for a beer. She didn't want to, since beer made her bloat, but after a day like today—

Olivia pitched forward as the taxi squeaked to a stop amid a cloud of dust.

"Which way?" asked the cabdriver.

Olivia strained to see where they were. "To the ranch house, I guess."

"Which way is that?"

"How should *I* know?"

The dust settled, and Olivia realized they sat at a fork in the road. She peered down one narrow road and saw a cluster of buildings and trees off in the distance. Down the other, more buildings and trees, a corral and horses. So which led to a bath?

Her cab fare was already in three figures. Did taking the wrong way really matter at this point?

Before she could decide, a horse and rider, galloping full-out, approached from the field of bluebonnets on the left. He must have seen the taxi.

"Maybe we can ask him." Olivia leaned out the window, fully expecting the man to stop. While she waited, she admired the sight of him bent over his magnificent horse, surging through the bluebonnets.

Her first real cowboy. Hat, jeans, boots and all. Unfortunately his hat obscured his face, leaving it in shadow. It was a white hat, so he must be one of the good guys.

The horse's mane and tail flew out in a straight line, just like in the movies. She could hear the rhythmic thunk of the hooves and see the muscles bunching in its glistening chest.

Mesmerized, Olivia stared at the progress of horse and rider galloping to her rescue. He'd rein in his horse, doff his hat and with a "Howdy, ma'am," welcome her to the ranch. Very impressive. Maybe this ranch idea wasn't so bad, after all.

Wishing she resembled Diana a bit more, Olivia checked her appearance in the cabbie's rearview mirror, cringed and attempted to finger comb her hair.

The pitter-patter of hooves changed to a rumbling thunder.

He isn't slowing down, Olivia realized at the precise moment the cabdriver began shouting in his mother tongue.

The hat still shaded the cowboy's face, but Olivia detected an expression of grim satisfaction as he aimed his horse straight at them. She gasped, inhaling grit. The horse tensed, then uncoiled its red length, soaring silently over the cab.

Olivia braced for a collision, for the sound of metal horseshoes striking metal car. The cabbie screamed; the horse grunted.

A shadow blocked the sun, then man and horse landed on the other side, galloping away.

Deep laughter trailed after them.

Stunned, Olivia listened to the hoofbeats fade.

The cabdriver, muttering in the same unrecognizable language, jerked the car into gear and floored it, taking the fork that led away from the corral. Away from the horseman.

Fine with her.

Olivia gazed out the back window until the maniacal cowboy was only a speck. Wouldn't the owner of Bluebonnet Ranch just love to hear about this?

No. There was no need to be a tattletale. The insolent rider probably expected her to go whining to the saint in charge, so she wouldn't.

Olivia smiled to herself. Now that she thought about it, she liked the cowboy's style. It confirmed her impression of Texas as an untamed frontier. Larger than life. Big, bold and brash.

Exactly like Diana D'Angelo.

Much struck, Olivia mulled this over as the cabbie rolled onto a gravel drive.

She could see at a glance that she'd come to the right place. Now that the huge trees didn't block the view, pickup trucks and a dressing trailer were visible, parked next to a long, single-story building that needed a paint job.

John Paul was his usual harried self: pointing, running his fingers through his lush fake hair, tugging on his clipped beard and issuing orders to eager minions.

Olivia stepped from the cab, expecting a delighted greeting.

"Good Lord, you took a cab?" John Paul came rushing over. "Why didn't you rent a car?"

"I don't drive," Olivia reminded him. He didn't either, she knew.

John Paul stuck his head inside the cab to check the meter. "Good Lord," he said again. "Go see that woman over there," he directed the scowling cabbie. The cabbie spat out words in the language he'd used since their encounter with the horse and rider.

John Paul smiled thinly. "She's the only one with money." He held up his hand rubbing his fingers together. "Mon-ey," he enunciated, jerking his thumb toward his assistant. Raising an eyebrow, he said, "Though it's a bit more than the usual petty-cash amount, isn't it Olivia, darling?"

Oops. Things must not be going well. "This is a bit more than the usual cab ride away from the airport. Why didn't you send someone for me?"

"Frankly, I forgot."

Olivia's eyes widened as John Paul demanded a receipt from the returning cabbie, who responded by dumping her suitcase on the gravel drive and escaping in a cloud of fumes.

They had *forgotten* her? She was the star. They couldn't shoot without her. How could they forget *her?*

"This place is barbaric." John Paul brought his fingers to his forehead and massaged his temples. "We're already several days behind."

"How can you be several days behind? We were only scheduled for three days—four max."

Mutely John Paul gestured toward the long building. "Look at it."

Olivia tilted her head. "It needs painting, so what? You knew you were going to have to paint."

"It needs a lot more than paint."

"*I* think it adds a rustic charm to the background."

John Paul shuddered.

"Besides, you don't have to paint it now. Wouldn't that be something Diana would have done later?" she asked, hoping that the suggestion wouldn't prompt a scene in which Diana actually wielded a brush.

Pounding hooves beat on the edges of her consciousness. She instinctively clutched at John Paul as she whipped her head around.

Her cowboy was bearing down on them.

Scrambling well out of his way, Olivia abandoned her suitcase.

The horse skirted around it, sending gravel flying. Reining in, the cowboy dismounted, striding toward them, anger visible in every long-limbed step he took.

Jeans had never looked so good. They fitted as if they'd been custom-crafted just for him. From the low-slung waist to the hems that exposed boots coated with a fine white dust, the man and his jeans were one.

The cowboy's worn boots crunched with hypnotic regularity on the gravel drive. Muscled legs swung in a loose but purposeful rhythm. The Texas sun glinted off a huge silver belt buckle that drew Olivia's attention as it dipped and swayed with the rocking motion of his hips.

She swallowed. "You say we're going to be here a few extra days?"

"Shh," John Paul hissed.

Olivia tore her eyes away from the buckle's undulations long enough to appreciate tapering Western-cut shirts for the first time. No extra material hiding a paunch. When a man wore one of those shirts, what you saw was what you got.

His loping gait brought him close enough for her to see the pearl snap buttons on the shirt and the pattern on his obligatory bandanna. He was also close enough for Olivia to get a good long look at his face, which was still shaded by a flint-colored hat.

Stopping, he tilted his head back slightly, and she saw his eyes, which raked her with one dismissing glance, then pinned their piercing glare on John Paul.

"You are not painting my bunkhouse blue." He glowered at John Paul for several seconds, then acknowledged her by touching his hat brim. "Ma'am."

He bobbed his head as he turned, striding back toward his horse.

"Mr. Chance!" John Paul called after him, a note of pleading in his voice. When there was no response, he stared at the sky. "I hope You're amused." Inhaling deeply, John Paul jogged after the retreating man. "Mr. Chance! If we could just talk? Don't get back on the horse!"

So that was Lucas Chance? The reckless horseman and Bluebonnet's owner were one and the same? Olivia revised her opinion of him, which she'd based solely on the saintly Lucas Chance described in the brochures.

Boy, was he tall, she marveled. She enjoyed the sight of John Paul trotting after him almost as much as she enjoyed watching the negligent sway of Lucas Chance's hips. Reaching his horse, a russet beauty, he patted it, then vaulted into the saddle.

John Paul stopped several feet away from the shifting hooves. "I'm thinking a nice gray-blue."

Lucas ignored him and trotted the horse toward her.

Olivia shrank back, caught herself and stopped. She wasn't afraid—this man wouldn't hurt her. However, she wasn't too sure about the horse.

Stopping midway across the drive, he pointed to her suitcase. "Better move that before something happens to it."

"Sure." She edged toward the case. Actually she'd hoped to snag a spare ranch hand into carrying it for her. The luggage wheels would be useless on the gravel. Unfortunately spare ranch hands were nowhere around. "Maybe you could call someone?"

The horse snorted and twitched.

Lucas patted its neck. "This isn't a hotel." With a touch of his hat brim, he cantered off, leaving Olivia in a haze of settling dust.

Across the drive, John Paul conferred with members of the set crew, who had brought him a board with varying patches of blue smeared on it.

Olivia looked down at her oatmeal linen pantsuit with the matching calfskin pumps and wondered if either would survive the trip. Grabbing the suitcase, she dragged it over the gravel.

"Is this the guest house?" She nodded to the building behind them.

"Guest house?" John Paul laughed. "There *is* no guest house."

"Okay," Olivia said evenly. "Where's my room?"

Everyone found this equally amusing. "In there with the rest of us." John Paul pointed to the long, one-story building he wanted to paint blue.

"The bunkhouse?"

"You got it."

"We're *all* in the bunkhouse?" she asked.

"Just like one big happy family." John Paul liked his creature comforts. Judging by his tone, he found them lacking.

It'd do him good to rough it for a couple of days. And this might be interesting, provided she could find someone to cart her suitcase over there. Olivia had never seen the inside of a bunkhouse and visualized a college dorm. It wouldn't hurt to soak up a little atmosphere.

"Let's go see if he'll accept this blue, instead of avoiding the issue by galloping away on his horse." John Paul and the crew walked off, leaving Olivia stranded with her suitcase.

Gritting her teeth, she propped the dusty case next to the stone walls of the ranch house, noting how the layered flat rocks and the uneven exterior would make an excellent background for photographs.

The house wasn't large, but the creamy stones were the same color as the boulders on the hills. Wooden beams were stained a deep brown, and spiky, dark green plants ringed the foundation. The perfect building for its environment.

Puzzled, she gazed after John Paul. And he wanted to paint the bunkhouse blue? What a mistake.

She caught up with him as he intercepted Lucas Chance, returning without his horse.

"This is more gray than blue. If we add any more charcoal, the whole effect will be dirty." John Paul smiled, one of the thin-lipped sarcastic smiles Olivia dreaded. "And we already have dirty."

Lucas Chance propped one hand on his hip. "No."

"We'll just paint these two sides of the building."

"Paint 'em white."

John Paul exhaled. "White is impossible."

"Why?"

"It wreaks havoc with the lighting. It's too bright, too harsh." He snapped his fingers. "Get me white." One of the set crew scurried away and returned with a large white square.

"Olivia." John Paul gestured imperiously. "Look at this." He held the square up to her face. "See what the sunlight does? Look around her eyes—wrinkles, dark circles. The color in her cheeks has leeched out. The lines around her mouth age her. She looks like a hag."

"Thanks a lot!"

"Quiet, Olivia. We can't have our actresses looking like wrinkled crones."

Olivia gazed at the silent man before her and found he was examining her with a thoroughness that brought warmth to her cheeks. She forced herself to meet his eyes and waited for the verdict.

"She looks okay to me."

How eloquent.

John Paul waved away the comment as he substituted the blue board for the white. "You have an untrained eye."

"I *like* his untrained eye," she said.

John Paul ignored her. "Now see this blue? It softens and diffuses the light. When we film, it will appear almost white. Notice how her crow's-feet are hardly visible."

Olivia made a mental note to slather on the moisturizer and slip John Paul the article she'd found on hair loss.

Lucas shook his head. "Not blue."

"Aside from its wonderful photographic properties, why blue, anyway?" Olivia asked.

John Paul looked heavenward. "Because of *Bluebonnet Ranch!*"

He *would* think that way. "You're keeping the same name for the Diana story line?"

"Yes." Now the ugly smile was aimed toward her. "You need to get out of the sun, dear. We mustn't freckle."

Olivia still smarted from his "hag" comments. "Oh, I forgot. Freckles aren't in my contract."

The smile thinned. "Neither are crow's-feet."

Lucas sauntered off, leaving Olivia regretting her squabbling with John Paul, who abandoned her at once to scurry after the tall rancher.

"Mr. Chance?" John Paul wasn't used to being ignored. Olivia knew an explosion was imminent.

"Luke." He threw the word over his shoulder.

"Luke, then. About the blue?"

"Nope."

"What about the ranch house?" Olivia said. Both men turned toward her. "Why not film against that?"

John Paul massaged his temples again. Olivia knew he wanted to tell her to stay out of the discussion but was going to pretend she didn't.

"The ranch house isn't Diana. We'll tape those scenes on a set." He opened his arms. "What we want is the feeling of vastness. The horses. Land. Wealth. We want a ranch that will be worth Diana and Megan fighting over."

Megan. The new ingenue. Olivia growled low in her throat. When she'd left New York, they'd already begun auditions.

"We want stock footage to insert in the coming weeks." He turned with a grimace masquerading as a smile. "But Luke, here, won't cooperate."

"Can you paint it blue and then repaint when you're ready to leave?" Olivia picked her way over the gravel.

John Paul eyed Luke, who shrugged. "Long as you can do it in two days."

"It is impossible to paint that—" John Paul gestured with contempt toward the bunkhouse "—film and repaint in two days!"

Luke shrugged again, but Olivia sensed his impatience.

"Luke, why only two days?" Olivia intervened before John Paul completely alienated him.

He turned his attention to her. She wished he'd take off that hat so she could get a good look at his entire face.

"First group of kids comes in two days."

"Kids? You mean the delinquents?" John Paul squeaked.

A muscle bulged in Luke's jaw, a sign that he was gritting his teeth.

John Paul obviously didn't notice. "You failed to inform us that criminals were due on the premises."

At the word "criminal," Luke flinched, and Olivia instinctively grabbed his arm. *I'm gonna punch that pansy right in the jaw.* She could hear his thought almost as if he'd breathed it into her ear.

"You didn't ask." Luke flexed his muscles but didn't shrug off her hand. "'Course it won't matter—you'll be gone."

Holding on to his arm was like gripping a metal pipe. John Paul owed her, big-time.

As the producer began a sputtering protest, Luke bent down and murmured to her, "Need some help with that suitcase?"

"Yes!" She exploded in relief at his quietly worded offer.

They left John Paul whining about contracts, Mr. Collingsworth, ungrateful ranch owners and the effect of overtime on production budgets.

"You can let go now," Luke said with dry amusement.

Olivia discovered she didn't want to let go, but could hardly cling to a virtual stranger who was not her leading man.

Luke and his boots efficiently crunched their way back to the abandoned suitcase. Olivia wobbled as her high heels stabbed through the rocky drive. She wended her way as quickly as she could, in imminent danger of twisting her ankle.

She wasn't quick enough. Luke stopped and silently watched her battle with the gravel before returning and offering her his steel bar of an arm again.

"They're not criminals," he said suddenly. "Not deep down."

John Paul's thoughtless comments had upset Luke more than she'd realized. He wasn't angry for himself—he was angry for the kids. "Unfortunately John Paul is very interested in shallow. Haven't you noticed?"

He may have smiled, but she didn't look quickly enough to catch it. John Paul obviously grated on him as much as he grated on John Paul. She suspected Luke's uninhibited ride had been to blow off steam.

They reached her suitcase, and Luke hauled it up to the porch. "You got any other shoes besides the ones you're wearing?"

"Yes, my running shoes." Olivia gratefully unlocked her suitcase and grabbed her shoes. She snatched off one pump and shifted her weight, wincing as the gravel bit into her foot.

"Hold on." Before she could guess his intention, Luke spanned her waist with his hands and lifted her onto the top step.

It happened so fast that she registered his touch only after he'd released her. The imprint of his hands stayed far longer than the time he'd held her.

He took the shoe from her nerveless fingers and placed it in the suitcase, gently pushing aside underwear. Olivia stared at the movements of his dark hand against her lingerie.

"Thanks." Her voice sounded rough. She cleared her throat and tossed her other pump at the suitcase. Luke caught it and placed it with the same care as he had the other one.

Olivia had shared dressing rooms with men. She'd matter-of-factly acted steamy love scenes wearing little more than a sheet or a skimpy negligee.

But the sight of Luke touching her underwear embarrassed her.

It *was* embarrassment she felt, wasn't it?

Olivia concentrated on tying her shoelaces, holding her breath until she heard the click of the latches on her suitcase.

"Ready?"

She nodded and hopped down before he could touch her again.

Now that she had proper shoes she could almost keep up with him.

"So how come you're late?"

Olivia was getting used to Luke's economical way of talking. "I'm not needed until they're all set up."

"What do you do?"

"I'm an actress. I play Diana D'Angelo on *Lovers and Liars.*" How long was it since she hadn't been recognized?

He gazed down at her. Olivia kept her profile to him. "You don't look like a star."

"So I've been told today. My ego's crushed."

"Sorry." She sensed his withdrawal after the terse apology.

"Hey, I know what you meant." She tugged on his arm. "Playing Diana is a job. I'm off duty now. I'll look like a star tomorrow after wardrobe and makeup get through. Add the hair and an attitude, and you won't recognize me."

There was silence after her babble. Luke didn't babble. Actually Olivia hadn't realized she did, either. In New York it was called small talk.

"I'd recognize you."

For some absurd reason, Olivia felt she'd just received the ultimate compliment.

She inhaled the dry, dusty air, thinking it was honest dirt and not city pollution.

There was peace to be found here. Quiet. Olivia took another breath, feeling tension drain from her. The stress of New York melted away.

She raised her head and saw the sky. Miles and miles of sky. And it was blue.

Like Luke's eyes.

Smiling to herself, she followed him into the bunkhouse.

CHAPTER THREE

"I'M SUPPOSED TO SLEEP in here?" Talk about returning to earth with a thud. If Olivia had ever entertained romantic thoughts of ranch life—and she most certainly hadn't—the sight of the bunkhouse interior would have cured her.

Rows of bunk beds stretched on either side of the long, one-room building. Midway down, sheets hanging from a rope divided the room, like the curtains separating first class from coach on an airplane.

Luke slid her suitcase inside the door with more force than necessary. "I don't understand you people. This isn't a dude ranch. I didn't ask you to come here."

"Didn't you?" She'd been ready to apologize until his last statement. "*Lovers and Liars* paid you for the right to use your ranch, didn't they?"

"Yes." The admission was a long time in coming.

"You and Mr. Collingsworth want the publicity, don't you?"

"Collingsworth thinks it'll help," Luke said grudgingly.

"So you're hardly allowing us to stay here out of the goodness of your heart." Olivia approached the curtains. "Did someone force you to sign the contract?"

"No one held a gun to my head, if that's what you're implying."

"I'm not implying anything. But this is—" she searched for words that wouldn't make her sound like a complete jerk "—a little more primitive than I was prepared for."

"It's a bunkhouse!" He gazed around. "It's clean, and you have a place to sleep. You knew you were coming to a ranch. What did you expect?"

Olivia was aware she was overreacting because she was hot, tired and dirty, and she'd been counting on a bath. She had no illusions about finding a hidden spa anywhere on the premises. Running water was the most she could hope for.

"I expected guest quarters." It seemed silly now, but she *had* thought she was going to a dude ranch. In the back of her mind, she'd even toyed with the idea of staying on for an extra day or two, since she wasn't currently taping any scenes on the show. Maybe even take some horseback riding lessons.

"For thirty people?" he sounded incredulous. "Do *you* have thirty spare bedrooms at your place?"

"Of course not. But according to the literature I read, you're used to having groups here."

"Yeah, and we spend a lot of time in tents."

"I can see why," Olivia muttered under her breath. "What about your ranch hands?"

"They've been known to sleep here on occasion. Never heard any complaints."

"Well, where are they now?"

"On spring roundup." He glared. "Matter of fact, I'd like to be with them, myself, instead of riding herd on you people."

Olivia glared back. "If you'd informed the production department that you lacked housing, they would've rented more trailers."

"And torn up the grass? No way. Besides, I wasn't expecting all these people."

"But surely you knew we were coming?"

Luke exhaled. "He said publicity pictures and exterior shots." Olivia guessed Luke referred to John Paul. "So I figured a couple of guys with cameras. Not—" he gestured mutely "—this."

Olivia could understand what had happened. John Paul probably assumed that Luke was familiar with production terms. John Paul probably also shared her dude-ranch fantasy, especially since he knew Luke regularly housed groups of people. But here?

"Is this where the kids stay?" she asked quietly.

Luke crossed his arms over his chest in the classic defensive position. "Yes."

"Both girls and boys sleep here—together?"

"No, not together," he said in a voice that told her he didn't appreciate criticism, implied or otherwise. "I hardly ever have girls. Only once, and the cook's wife and sister came to stay."

"You don't have a wife of your own?" Olivia asked, but she already knew the answer. The interior of the bunkhouse screamed for a woman's touch. She didn't know any woman who could resist the call, herself included.

"No!"

Sore subject. "I guess that would make it awkward for you to take in girls," she said smoothly, reaching out and pulling back the white sheet. As she suspected, the female crew members had staked their claim on this end of the bunkhouse. A corner of Olivia's mouth tilted upward. Close to the bathroom, such as it was.

She could see sinks and showers through the open door, and the rest she could see reflected in the mirrors.

The Ritz it was not.

John Paul must have had a fit, which would explain the animosity between the producer and Luke.

She turned to face him. He stood, arms still crossed, legs apart, blocking the late-afternoon sun.

"You'll find bedding and towels in the cabinets next to the bathroom."

Olivia sighed.

"You *do* know how to make your own bed, don't you?"

Rather than answer him, Olivia snapped, "You're enjoying this, aren't you?"

He unfolded his arms and gripped the doorjamb. "No, ma'am, I am not. But you'll be gone in two days." He stepped out into the sunlight. "Or else."

"Or else what?" she called after him.

"Or else you'll share with the boys who're coming in on Saturday." He touched his hat brim and sauntered off.

Share? With *boys?* Would these be the "troubled youths" the brochure euphemistically referred to? Was John Paul aware of this?

Olivia suspected that Luke had told him, but that John Paul didn't actually believe it would happen.

Olivia believed, and she scurried to wheel her suitcase behind the sheet curtain.

Naturally all the lower bunks were taken, with suitcases and incredible amounts of junk stuffed under them.

Olivia examined each of the top bunks, choosing as hers the one with the least stained ticking.

This was horrible. As she understood it, Mr. Collingsworth contributed to Luke's program. Well, it was time for Collingsworth to spring for new mattresses. Ha-ha-ha.

Olivia groaned and sat on somebody's bunk. It groaned, too.

No, she wasn't being a good sport.

Yes, she was giving the impression she was a spoiled star.

No, she wasn't sorry.

Yes, she was.

Luke was coping the best he could. And John Paul had had virtually no preparation time. She needed to hurry up and get settled, then see what she could do to help.

The cabinets held a quantity of sheets and towels, all in the same graying white. As she grabbed a stack, Olivia was assailed with childhood memories. This bunkhouse was actually better than some of the seedy hotels she'd stayed in with her parents when they'd been on the regional-theater circuit.

Leaning close to the mattress, Olivia sniffed gingerly. There it was, the familiar stale and sour smell of ancient bedding. Hard on that came the bittersweet memory of vanilla.

Olivia tucked in the corner of the double thickness of sheets she'd wrapped around the thin mattress.

Vanilla. Her mother would soak a handkerchief in vanilla extract and put it in Olivia's pillowcase in an attempt to camouflage the smell of the bedding.

Her mother never used perfume, neither the heavy rich perfumes of the big stars, nor the tinny synthetic florals of the lesser lights. Vanilla was wholesome. Vanilla was supposed to mean home. A mother who spent afternoons in the kitchen baking, not a mother who spent days as an extra on a movie set.

And a father who held a regular job. In one place. Not a father who sometimes left his family behind when he went on location so Olivia could attend enough school to comply with the law. But that was only when there was no tutor on the set. And since there was usually a tutor on the set, separations from her father hadn't been all that frequent.

However, staying in cheap lodgings had been. And the vanilla had never really fooled her.

Olivia Faraday had worked long and hard to keep from ever being forced to stay in a place like this again. To keep her parents—still waiting for their big break—from ever staying in a place like this again.

Olivia had the character of Diana to thank for everything. Diana was her security, the only security she'd ever known. Diana had allowed her to put down roots. Diana had paid for the brand-new mattress Olivia had bought with her first paycheck. So for Diana's sake, Olivia would suppress the memories and stay in the bunkhouse until Saturday.

But just before she went in search of John Paul, Olivia squirted her pillowcase with the heavy perfume of a big star.

THEY WEREN'T FINISHED by Saturday.

At noon, a tight-lipped Luke emerged from the Bluebonnet van. He'd driven into Austin to meet the group of kids and had now returned.

Olivia stood in the shade of a photography light reflector and tried not to sweat.

"I told you people to be out of here by the time I got back!" His gaze flicked over the equipment, eyes narrowing at the two extra trailers that hadn't been there when he'd left for the airport. "Is it my imagination, or are there even more of you?"

"Mr. Chance." John Paul, who hadn't successfully been able to call him Luke, beckoned. "Some of the media have heard about you." John Paul emphasized "media." Olivia doubted Luke cared.

Wheel ruts marred the grassy shoulders of the gravel drive. When Olivia had pointed out the damage to John Paul, he'd retorted, "It'll be a lot worse when the entire crew is on location."

He'd been quivering with excitement. The *Lovers and Liars* publicity mill had been hard at work, and a couple of the soap fan magazines had tried to scoop each other on the new direction the ailing soap was headed.

Olivia had spent the wee hours of the morning donning full Diana makeup. The clothing was more difficult. It hadn't yet been decided whether Diana was truly going Western or just adopting the look for a few weeks.

They'd been working since before dawn, but even so, Olivia had known it would be impossible to finish by noon, their Luke-imposed deadline.

John Paul was unconcerned, telling her Luke would change his mind when he heard about the opportunity for extra publicity.

Sure he would.

As far as Olivia could tell, Luke didn't care about anything but those kids. Curious, she studied their sullen faces in the van windows.

They were not faces she'd like to meet in a dark alley, and frankly, they looked as if they'd seen a dark alley or two in their young lives.

She made plans to move her things to the new makeup trailer, where she'd thankfully sleep on the floor if John Paul didn't finish today.

"You want to borrow *what?*" Luke thundered, drawing her attention.

Olivia had never heard him raise his voice before. John Paul must have asked to borrow the horse. He'd made noises in that direction this morning, and she'd tried to discourage him. Horses were large, smelly animals that commanded her utmost respect.

From a distance.

Olivia left the skimpy shade and walked closer to the interested knot of observers.

"A horse." John Paul laughed and clapped Luke on the shoulder for the benefit of the photographers. Olivia had seen him in action before. "You know, Trigger? Mr. Ed?" The reporters and photographers chuckled.

Luke didn't.

John Paul's hand slid away. "How about that auburn one you ride?"

"Vulcan?" Slowly Luke shook his head. "Nobody rides Vulcan but me."

Vulcan? Through Olivia's mind flashed the image of Luke and Vulcan soaring over her cab. She breathed a sigh of relief.

"John Paul? Why don't I just sit on the fence right about here." Olivia clomped over to an area opposite the bunkhouse. Wardrobe had provided her with jeans and a sky-blue shirt, but no boots. She'd borrowed a pair from a painter on the set crew. "I'll sit on top, they can take pictures from this side, and the bunkhouse will be visible in the background."

The bunkhouse was something to behold. Luke had prevailed—it was white, but a huge spray of bluebonnets had been painted on it. Surprisingly Luke had said nothing.

The crew members and photographers clambered over the fence and began to set up.

"Yes, yes, Olivia, darling, but this is a *ranch,*" John Paul fretted. "People will expect horses and cows and that sort of thing." He looked around. "Though we're a bit thin on livestock...."

"I keep telling you, it's roundup time," Luke said, annoyed. "But you can have all the horses and cattle you can handle as long as it gets you out of here."

"Mr. Chance?" called a reporter. "Would you step closer to Miss Faraday?"

Olivia had wondered just how long it would take the photographers to discover Luke. With his long, lean good looks and a set of incredible cheekbones, he was a natural model.

Besides, what was a ranch without a cowboy?

John Paul, no fool, had retreated out of camera range.

Luke squinted at the clutch of photographers and frowned. When he realized their intention, he held up his hand and backed off. "Hey, I don't want any part of this."

"Luke, come here," Olivia ordered.

He looked surprised at her tone, but complied. "I don't want my picture taken."

"Yes, you do, and I'll tell you why," she said in low voice. "Now that they've got the idea of photographing a cowboy, if you won't let them take your picture, they'll try to find someone who will. He'll have to be tall and on the lean side, because the camera adds ten pounds. Then when—*if*—they decide one of the available males within the immediate vicinity qualifies, they'll have to outfit him. I guarantee wardrobe didn't bring male clothes. They'll either make do and grumble about it, or send someone back to Austin, which, as you know, is a three-hour round trip. By the time they're ready to shoot, it'll be sunset and the light will be gone. So they'll call it a day and try again tomorrow."

Olivia propped an elbow against the wooden fence and stared up at him. "We'll be here until Sunday at least."

"Not if I can help it." He was irritated and with good reason.

"Have you been able to help it so far?"

Luke glanced at the photographers. "Obviously not."

"So let them take your picture, and they'll leave."

Luke appeared to mull over her suggestion. When he faced her again, he wore a bemused expression. "Shouldn't I change my clothes or something?"

"You look fine." More than fine. Just as fine as she did, and she'd spent an hour in makeup and another thirty minutes on her hair. And then they covered it with a hat.

And Luke, who had done nothing more than shower and shave, looked great.

Olivia sighed. Men. Life wasn't fair.

"John Paul!" Luke shouted at her producer. "Find Simon and ask him to let those kids out of the van before they burn up. He can take them to the chow house for some lemonade."

Luke took two long-legged strides toward her. Olivia could already detect the click and whir of cameras. She held in her stomach.

"What am I supposed to do?"

She smiled. "Just be you."

"If I was being me, I'd be drinking lemonade right now."

Olivia threw back her head and laughed. It was a genuine laugh, but she was completely aware of how it would appear in a photograph.

Luke grinned and leaned his elbows on the fence. He ducked his head and pushed his hat back off his forehead, lifting one booted foot to rest on the lower railing.

Classic cowboy.

A fraction of a second later, Olivia had matched his pose, knowing it was a good one.

The photographers scurried to capture the pair on film.

Luke gazed out at them. "Shouldn't I be doing something else?"

"You could tell me how John Paul talked you into letting flowers get painted on the bunkhouse."

"That wasn't his idea."

Luke shifted until he was facing her, one elbow still on the fence.

"It wasn't?" Unobtrusively Olivia turned toward him. As long as she could keep him relaxed and talking, she knew there would be some good shots.

"I got to talking to one of your crew, Tom. He grew up in Lubbock, and we traded some stories."

"I know Tom." She gestured to her feet. "I'm wearing his boots."

Luke favored her with another brief grin. Olivia grinned back, liking the way the skin folded alongside his mouth when he smiled.

"Yeah, Tom's an okay guy. He came up with the bluebonnet idea to break up the white. He let me see what that white paint does to the light meters. Really pegs them out."

Olivia had suspected Luke would be reasonable if John Paul had asked, rather than argued and demanded. But arguing and demanding was John Paul's style, and why not? It worked well in New York.

"Tom said if I didn't like it, they could paint over it." Luke studied the bunkhouse. "I like it. Tom knows his bluebonnets."

"Excuse me," interrupted a photographer. "Could we have Miss Faraday sit on the fence now? We're ready for closeups."

Olivia hooked her boot heel on the railing, then felt Luke's hands around her waist as he lifted her up.

"Hold it!" cried the photographer.

For an eternity, she endured the spreading warmth of his touch, which made her forget time and place. There were several exposures of her with her mouth hanging open, until she remembered she was being photographed and pasted a laughing expression on her face.

Her knees pressed against the solidly muscled wall of his chest. Rough wood pricked her palms where she gripped the railing.

Luke's face was inches away. Even though she sat on the fence, she was just about eye level with him.

They stared at each other. Olivia was afraid to move, afraid Luke would sense her disquiet. She was drawn to this laconic rancher, but for him to know it wasn't a good idea.

She watched his eyes study her and warm. "You're just a little bit of a thing, aren't you?"

Olivia suddenly wondered if Luke preferred little bits of women or women in larger hunks.

His thumbs began a meticulous inventory of her ribs, causing sensations somewhere between a tickle and—

"Kiss her!"

That would never do. She made it a practice never to kiss an actor she wanted to kiss. Unless she was dating him, of course, but an actor in a scene? Not good. And right now, Luke was an actor in a scene, whether he realized it or not. "Hey, you guys. Knock it off." She tried to wriggle out of his grasp.

Luke didn't let go.

Olivia glanced at him in surprise. "Oh, no." She knew that look. *What a wonderful idea,* it said. "You don't have to kiss me."

"I want to." His lips curved.

"They have plenty of good shots." Kissing him would be a monumental mistake.

"I want to, anyway."

"It isn't necessary. Really."

"I'm going to." He moved closer, still smiling.

Olivia's heart pounded. Everyone was entitled to a mistake or two. "Well, if you insist."

"I insist." His hand left her waist and grasped her nape.

"Remember, I'm Diana."

"I know who you are."

"It won't be a real kiss, you understand." Her voice sounded funny.

"Yes, it will."

And it was.

There was no rough country-boy technique about him. This cowboy knew his way around a pair of lips.

Their hat brims collided, and Olivia's slid down her back.

Hoots and whistles from the photographers didn't affect Luke at all.

After a moment, they didn't affect Olivia, either.

She clung to him to keep her balance.

Then she clung to him to keep him close.

This was no studio kiss, mindful of camera angles, smeared makeup and squashed features.

This was a cowboy kiss. She tasted sun and heat and salt. The waxy scent of her photographic makeup mingled with leather and cotton and dry Texas outdoors.

Her lipstick smeared over the roughening stubble of Luke's beard as he teased her lips apart.

It was only when his tongue sought hers that Olivia broke the kiss. Turning her face aside, she kept both hands on his shoulders as she pushed him away and slid off the fence in one smooth movement.

"I think that's enough of that." Avoiding his gaze, she ran a shaky hand through her hair.

"I don't," he said, reaching for her.

She intercepted his hand and shook it. "Careful. Don't forget the photographers."

"I don't give a damn about the photographers." He gripped her hand, preventing her from pulling away.

Olivia tried a light laugh and risked a glance at him. "You have lipstick on your mouth."

"I don't—"

"Luke."

He acknowledged her serious tone by dropping her hand.

"You kissed Diana. For the cameras. I'm not Diana," she said as the makeup artist rushed over to repair her lipstick. "I'm Olivia."

"Then who kissed me back?" he murmured.

"Powder!" called the makeup woman as Olivia felt herself blush.

"People, that was just great. Fabulous, Olivia, dear," gushed John Paul. "Mr. Chance—" John Paul clasped his hands together "—we're, ah, ready for the horses now."

Horses? "Don't they have enough pictures?" Olivia asked.

John Paul regarded her, eyes narrowed. "Can you bend in those jeans, dear? We wouldn't want to cut off your circulation."

"Hey!" Luke cut off their sniping with a shout, waved his arms, then jogged toward the ranch house.

Olivia stared after him, trying to see what had upset him.

"Olivia?" John Paul tugged on her arm. She ignored him.

"Olivia, can you sit on a horse in those jeans?"

She shrugged off his hand. "What's going on?"

A few of the photographers had moved their equipment. She could see Luke gesture angrily and shake his head. Grabbing the railing, Olivia hoisted herself up and strained to see more.

The boys from the van must have finished their lemonade and were now gathered under the pecan tree in front of the ranch house. Luke stood between them and the photographers.

"What have you done, John Paul?" She jumped down from the fence.

John Paul pulled out a big paisley silk square and mopped his neck and forehead. "Nothing."

Olivia waved away the hairstylist, who approached with brush and comb, and planted her oversize cowboy hat back on her head. "If you won't tell me, I'll find out for myself."

"Don't concern yourself. We need you over here to set up the horse shots." He pointed toward the far side of the bunkhouse, which was doubling as the barn. There hadn't been time to paint the barn.

Olivia whirled on her heel and stomped off in her borrowed boots. What had John Paul done to make Luke so angry? she wondered. Within moments, she was in earshot of the argument.

"There was nothing in the contract about taking pictures of the kids!"

"What harm can it do?" asked one of the reporters. "They want to have their pictures taken, don't you, guys?"

Eight wary but interested faces stared back at him.

Head bands were still popular among young males, Olivia noticed, along with earrings and wispy first mustaches. The quintessentially urban baggy T-shirts, jeans and untied tennis shoes contrasted with the Western dress of Luke and the ranch hands. Olivia could see what appealed to the photographers. She could also understand how Luke felt. He was in an awkward position, and it was their fault.

"Miss Faraday?" A reporter had noticed her. "Can we get a couple of shots with you and the boys?"

"Uh..." Olivia hesitated, looking to Luke for guidance, but he was talking with Simon, the ranch hand who had driven in the van with him.

"Move it, dear." John Paul accompanied his whispered command with an ungentle push. "The publicity will be worth a fortune."

Two reporters were now interviewing Luke, so Olivia complied. It would be excellent publicity for them all.

Luke wanted publicity; wasn't that why he agreed to let them film *Lovers and Liars* here? He stood back, arms crossed, apparently agreeing to allow the photographers to include the boys in the pictures.

"How did you hear about the Bluebonnet Ranch program, Miss Faraday?" asked a reporter from one of the soap magazines.

"One of our sponsors, Collingsworth Industries, supports it," she replied, pleased with herself for working in the name.

"And you became involved because of them," the reporter prompted.

"Yes." Olivia wasn't sure exactly what the press had been told or what her position was supposed to be.

John Paul came to her rescue. "The cast of *Lovers and Liars* frequently donates their time to help worthy causes." He chatted on in that pseudoconfiding tone designed to seduce the media. Olivia smiled and presented her "sweet side" to the photographers.

"Miss Faraday, Bettina Lynne, of *Soap Bubbles.*" A woman who wore a hot-pink wool suit, yet still managed to look cool, took Olivia's elbow. "We'd like to ask you some questions on camera for airing this weekend."

Soap Bubbles was a weekly show featuring news from the world of soaps. Although Olivia was no stranger to the program, it had been awhile since she'd appeared in a segment. She expected John Paul to come with her, but he was still talking to other reporters.

It was okay. She knew the drill. Bettina positioned them so the sun wasn't in their eyes and turned to face her cameraman. Olivia waited quietly.

"Bettina Lynne, here on location at Bluebonnet Ranch. With me—" she cued Olivia, who moved into the frame "—is Olivia Faraday, who plays Diana D'Angelo on *Lovers and Liars.*" Bettina turned from the camera to her. "Tell me, Olivia, will we be seeing a new direction for Diana in the upcoming weeks?" She tilted the microphone toward Olivia.

Olivia smiled and answered in as vaguely truthful a manner as she could. It was always best to keep on the vague side, because things were never certain in the soap world.

Besides, at this point, it looked as though she might be headed for a coma. She hoped that would change.

"Tell us about the camping trip."

What camping trip? Two heartbeats went by—an eternity in television. "There's certainly some beautiful country around here for camping, isn't there?" *What camping trip?*

Out of camera range she signaled Bettina for another question. Bettina smiled. Evilly. "Come now, Olivia. Don't be modest. Folks—" Bettina addressed the camera "—Olivia Faraday is going along on one of Bluebonnet Ranch's famous wilderness camping trips."

She was? What wilderness camping trip? What publicity stunt had John Paul cooked up now?

Still smiling her evil smile, Bettina turned back to Olivia. "And we never would have known about it if a little bird hadn't tipped us off."

Olivia wanted to wring a certain little bird's neck. She couldn't disagree on camera. That was an unbreakable rule. One never disagreed for the record. She couldn't even look at John Paul—or Luke. The camera was focused on her face and would catch the shift of her eyes. She'd appear uncertain and Bettina would smell blood.

"Bettina, I think it's important to remember what's important here." That sounded stupid. "The boys. The boys are important. Luke has provided them with a wonderful opportunity, and I'm just doing what I can to help." *Help!* she screamed silently.

"How long have you been volunteering at Bluebonnet Ranch?"

"Oh..." Olivia shook her head, forgetting about her hat. Shaking her head and running her fingers through her hair was a standard Diana move. Olivia wanted to use it to stall for time, but couldn't while wearing the cowboy hat. "I don't know..." She laughed. "It seems like only yesterday that I first drove through the Bluebonnet gate."

This was a hideous interview. Where was John Paul?

Bettina, winking slyly at the camera, leaned closer. "Tell us, are things heating up between you and Lucas Chance?"

With a sinking sensation so strong Olivia was afraid she might actually be sick on camera, she said, "We're just good friends." She had absolutely no doubt that her voice would be dubbed over a picture of Luke kissing her.

She'd better warn him.

She'd also better remind him that she hadn't wanted him to kiss her.

But of course, that would be lying.

And he'd know it.

CHAPTER FOUR

BARELY LISTENING to Bettina wrap the segment, Olivia scanned the crowd for Luke. He'd been busy with the reporters; maybe he hadn't heard her interview.

She saw him at once, mounted on Vulcan. He stared down at her, his eyes glacial, his jaw set.

He'd heard.

As Vulcan snorted and pawed the gravel, Olivia thought that perhaps telling Bettina she and Luke were "good friends" had been a bit optimistic.

"Over here, Miss Faraday!"

Olivia gratefully looked away from Luke. It was apparent to her that he despised them all, and with some justification. She felt guilty and uncomfortable and wished John Paul would quit pandering to the media. Of course that *was* his job. And he did it very well. But they should leave and let Luke get on with his program.

The photographers clustered around the boys. With so much attention focused on them, all but one of the boys had thawed and willingly posed for pictures. Sighing, Olivia approached the group. Maybe she could pose for a couple of quick shots and then the reporters would leave.

As she walked nearer, several of the youths murmured among themselves, nudging and pointing at her.

Even the boy who hung back next to the tree stared at her.

Ah, she'd been recognized. She slipped into Diana mode by tossing her head and lifting her chin.

"Hey, you on TV?" The tallest of the boys called to her, the hot afternoon sun glinting off the silver earring he wore.

"Yes," Olivia answered cheerfully. "I play Diana D'Angelo on *Lovers and Liars.*" The entire time she spoke, she was aware of the photographers waiting for their shot and the reporters waiting for anything to report.

And she was aware of Luke, glaring down at her from his throne on Vulcan.

"Man, I told you she was on TV." The boy grinned and postured for his compatriots.

"What you be doin' here?" the shorter, tougher, hairier youth next to him asked her.

Olivia thought of him as the leader. The others had been watching to see his reaction.

"Turn this way... That's good. Hold it." Cameras whirred and clicked.

As she complied, Olivia answered the boy. "Today we're taking some publicity photos. Later on we're going to be filming a story here."

"And until then, Miss Faraday will be working with you here on the ranch," added Bettina.

Hadn't that woman left yet? Olivia didn't know—and didn't want to know—where she got her information.

"Doing what?" asked another reporter.

"Let's not exaggerate my contribution to the Bluebonnet program," Olivia said, trying to keep the trepidation out of her voice. *Where was John Paul?* How could he put her in this position? Was it too much to ask him to keep her informed?

"I think taking two weeks off from *Lovers and Liars* to volunteer your precious time is worth mentioning," Bettina gushed, her eyes sparkling malevolently.

Two weeks off? Bettina suspected something. Frankly, Olivia did, too. Two weeks? What was going on?

"We need a horse!" someone called.

"Can we get Diana to show the kids how to saddle a horse?"

Olivia rolled her eyes as she was referred to as Diana. It happened all the time, and usually she accepted it as part of being closely identified with a popular character. But right now, she was very conscious of the silent, disapproving figure on the big, red horse.

"Does Diana know how to saddle a horse?" Luke asked in a voice as dry as Texas dust.

Olivia cringed at the sarcasm. No, she didn't know how to saddle a horse. And she didn't care to learn.

But to be found lacking at just this moment was more than she could stand. She signaled the makeup woman for powder so she could avoid looking at Luke. Her timing was horrible, because it allowed the publicist and John Paul to answer the media for her.

"Miss Faraday generally doesn't advertise her charity work, but in this case, she'd like to draw people's attention to this wonderful program. She feels strongly that..."

Olivia listened in growing dread as John Paul and the publicist outlined her "involvement" with Bluebonnet Ranch. They were stretching the truth so far it was about to rip.

Her smile muscles ached. John Paul was a talented man, but he had a habit of tangling truth and illusion and leaving someone else to untie the knot.

"...wilderness camping trip."

Olivia tuned back in. What was this camping business? She hadn't agreed to go camping. Mentally noting to instruct her agent to include an approval clause for personal appearances in her next contract, Olivia interrupted the flow of publicity pap. "John Paul, the boys haven't had an opportunity to get settled. Let's finish the pictures now."

Someone snorted—no, some*thing* snorted.

A horse. A dappled gray horse that Luke, astride Vulcan, led toward her. The boys, urban to the core, jumped backward, then tried to pretend they hadn't been startled.

Olivia, heart in her throat, stood her ground.

The horse was big, twitchy and smelly. And Vulcan's glare matched Luke's.

"Wh-what's its name?" Olivia was horrified to hear the quiver in her voice. She stole a glance up at Luke.

"Her name's Star."

Oh, he was angry. Others might put his reticence down to shy cowboy overawed by big city folk, but Olivia knew better.

"Did you hear that?" gushed John Paul. "How appropriate! The horse's name is Star," he repeated for the press.

Swallowing, Olivia forced herself to reach out to pat the animal. But where should she touch it? Would it bite her? Kick her? Demand sugar or carrots, neither of which she had?

Trickles of sweat seeped through her shirt. Great. Wouldn't that look lovely in the photographs. Why hadn't she worn the plaid, instead of the pale blue?

Star reared her head, and Olivia snatched back her hand.

"She's being temperamental, just like a real star," Luke drawled with a wicked gleam in his eye.

As if Olivia didn't have enough to worry about, Luke was obviously going to be disagreeable until she had an opportunity to explain the rules of being interviewed, how even the most innocent statements could be twisted.

Luke held the horse while Olivia was positioned for an interminable series of photographs, usually pretending to show the boys how to tighten some strap on the saddle. Even the watchful boy by the tree edged closer.

Between her anxiety over the horse, her awareness of Luke's anger and disgust at her own part in playing along with John Paul's publicity madness, Olivia developed a whopper of a headache.

"Now get on the horse," someone suggested.

Olivia froze. *Get on the horse?* Whose idea was that? She was *not* going to get on the horse.

At precisely that moment, Star shied and swished her tail, flicking Olivia across the face. As her eyes streamed, she heard laughter and the cooing of the makeup artist, who rushed to repair the horsey damage. She also heard Luke's soothing murmurs, but he was talking to the horse. It figured.

Her mascara restored, Olivia laughed lightly, to show there were no hard feelings. "Talk about being brushed off." The photographers chuckled, but didn't move away.

No hope of escape. They still expected her to mount the blasted horse. Olivia turned her back to them, her eyes clenched shut. Deep breaths. Focus.

She wasn't an animal lover. Because of her nomadic childhood, she'd never owned a pet, and later she'd never wanted one.

Before coming to Bluebonnet Ranch, she'd flirted with the idea of taking riding lessons. Now, she wanted a stand-in.

Surely John Paul would rescue her. Taking a deep, steadying breath, Olivia opened her eyes.

The horse was still there. So was Luke. "C'mon up," he said.

Staring straight ahead, Olivia wiped her hands on her jeans. What did she do now? The stirrup was a long way from the ground. Her eyes began to tear again. Blinking rapidly, she looked up at Luke.

She was a fraud, and they both knew it. She was also a scared fraud and wanted him to know that, too. *Please help me,* she pleaded silently. Her big brown eyes had been described as "speaking" eyes. Well, they were shouting now.

The remote disdain faded from Luke's expression. He regarded her for what seemed forever, then sighed faintly and dismounted.

"This side," he directed. "I'll give you a leg up."

Olivia joined him on the other side of the horse, Star's body shielding them from the photographers.

"What do I do?" she mouthed.

"You get on the horse."

"How?"

He gazed at her in disbelief.

"I've never been on a horse before!" she confessed.

"For the love of—" Biting off the rest, he bent and cupped his hands. "Put your foot here— No, the other one."

Olivia balanced a hand on his shoulder. "Won't I hurt you?"

"Naw. You're too skinny."

Skinny? What happened to "a little bit of a thing?" She said, "Not on camera." If he only knew how hard she worked to keep "skinny."

"Grab hold of the saddle horn. The big bump," he added sarcastically when she hesitated.

"I *know* what a saddle horn is!"

"You didn't know which side of a horse to mount."

Olivia ignored him, wedged her oversize boot in his hand and pulled on the saddle horn. She flung her other leg over the horse's back and by some miracle landed in the saddle.

Star sidestepped and Olivia clung. Luke adjusted the stirrup on one side as her boot slid off her foot and plopped to the ground on the other.

His lips curved as he placed her foot in the stirrup and retrieved her boot. Olivia sat very, very still.

"Don't worry," he said, pushing the boot back on her foot. "I won't let anything happen to you."

She managed a weak smile. The ground seemed very far away.

Star turned her head as if to check out Olivia. Feeling a friendly gesture was called for, Olivia gingerly patted the horse's neck and felt the neck muscles quiver in response. Was that good or bad? Star's ears twitched. Could she hear Olivia's pounding heart?

Luke swung onto Vulcan and retrieved Star's reins with an ease Olivia envied.

For the next hour she clenched her legs around her poor horse. With Luke's constant encouragement, she managed to relax enough to release her death grip on the saddle horn, but compensated by squeezing her legs. They began to ache long before it was time to dismount.

The afternoon melted away, the lengthening shadows intriguing the photographers, who were inclined to be arty when they had the chance.

At last the photographers asked for one final setup with Olivia and Luke riding off into the sunset. What a cliché, a weary Olivia thought.

Luke reached for her reins. "Which direction are we heading?"

Olivia shaded her eyes under her hat. "Go west, young man."

He favored her with one of his rare smiles and cantered toward the west. Star followed without any encouragement whatsoever. Olivia bounced until she thought her teeth would fall out.

"Sl-slow down!" Certain parts of her anatomy—parts of which she was very fond—were numb.

"Relax and try to find the horse's rhythm," Luke suggested.

"I know *exactly* where the horse's rhythm is!" Olivia gritted her teeth as her bottom jounced against the saddle. "And it isn't doing me any good at all."

Luke shook his head, but slowed Vulcan. Star trotted alongside.

"Thanks," she said, though she was certain her spine would never be the same.

Luke didn't even look at her. In fact, he'd barely spoken to her during the photography session. It was obvious that soap-opera actresses weren't on his top-ten list of interesting women.

"Also thanks for helping me with the horse," she added, trying to make peace.

"Anything to get you people gone."

She'd ignore the unfriendliness in his voice. She was feeling grouchy herself. "Listen, while we're out here, fill me in on this wilderness camping trip. John Paul didn't tell me anything about it."

Luke squinted into the distance, and for a moment, Olivia thought he wouldn't answer. "Usually I have the boys here for a month at a time," he said at last. "For the first couple of weeks, they get acquainted with me, with the routine here and learn how to take care of their horses."

"They learn to ride?"

"Yep." He slid a glance her way. "Most catch on faster than you, though."

"I haven't fallen off yet," Olivia pointed out.

"There's still time."

Olivia squeezed her legs tighter. Luke continued, "Halfway through the month, we take off and camp. In addition to taking care of his own gear and horse, everybody has a job he does for the good of the group. It's a real job. A real responsibility. He messes up, and we all suffer."

"Suffer?" Olivia didn't like the sound of that.

"Not too much, but enough to make it count." Luke shifted in the saddle. "I have safeguards, but they're hidden. I forget about 'em unless somebody's honestly hurting."

"Do...do people get hurt?"

"Sometimes."

"Hurt, as in blood?"

"Sometimes."

Olivia couldn't believe his casual attitude. She couldn't think of anything to say.

He saw her face. "They're safer out there—" he swept his in a wide arc to indicate the land around them "—than they are where they live."

"I see."

"No, you don't." Luke reined in Vulcan. Star stopped without any signal from Olivia.

"You've met Collingsworth, right?" Luke asked.

Olivia nodded.

"Since I can't be here and in New York at the same time, he works with the Bluebonnet Foundation to identify the kids who'd be good candidates for the program. Usually they've had some minor skirmish with the law or they've started skipping school or hanging around with the wrong crowd, that sort of thing. I don't like to take them much older than fourteen. I notice I've got a couple of fifteen-year-olds this time, but this a special case."

"How so?" Star dropped her head and munched some grass. Olivia relaxed and winced at the ache in her leg muscles.

"It's spring break for them, for one thing. And beginning of roundup for me." Luke sighed and rubbed the back of his neck. "But their school counselors were convinced these kids were going to drop out of school, so we're trying a two-week experiment."

"You think it'll help?"

"Hope so."

In the distance a tiny John Paul waved for them to come in. Olivia almost wished Luke would ignore him. Things would be a lot simpler if one could ignore John Paul.

Luke made a clicking sound with his tongue and turned the horses back toward the ranch house. "I show the boys a different kind of life. Let them know they have choices, that they don't have to be trapped on the streets."

"But they'll go back to the same pressures, the same people, the same streets." Olivia knew how it was. Sometimes she thought *Lovers and Liars* was the whole world. Although she felt refreshed after vacations, the feeling never lasted.

"Those kids won't be the same. It changes you out there." He nodded to the distant hills. "You learn real quick what's important. You take care of your horse, or you can't ride. You don't keep up with the group, and you're on your own for food. Things like that. Basic survival stuff. I don't have them with me for long, and I don't want them to forget."

Olivia had been here only a few days and knew the memory would stay with her. It was so...different. She inhaled, the mesquite-tinged smoke from the cook-house teasing her nostrils. Barbecue. Her mouth watered. She'd eaten more meat in the past two days than she'd eaten in the past two months.

They were nearly back to the gravel drive outside the ranch buildings. Photographers were packing their equipment, quickly slipping into cars. Olivia saw the *Lovers and Liars* crew hauling their gear out of the bunkhouse. That was right—they had to vacate the bunkhouse now that the boys had arrived. She guessed the crew would drive to a hotel in Austin for the night.

Was she supposed to stay here until the camping trip? In the bunkhouse? Surely not. Olivia scanned the area for John Paul. He really should have asked her first. Scheduling public appearances was one thing, a two-week chunk of her time was something else. "I have to warn you, I'm not much of a camper," Olivia admitted, suspecting that Luke could figure that out. "But I want you to know that I'll do my best."

"At what?"

"At camping, of course." John Paul may have volunteered her without asking her first, but Olivia wasn't going to shy away from a commitment.

"You're not going on any camping trip," Luke stated as if there had never been any question of her going.

"But—"

"Watch it. You're starting to believe your own publicity."

"You think this is all a publicity stunt?" Olivia accused as they rode across the gravel to the bunkhouse.

Luke reached for her reins. "Isn't it?"

"No!" Olivia denied. "If they said I'll be here, then I'll be here." She waved as Bettina drove past. Thank goodness the woman was gone.

"You're not camping with us." He dismounted and looked up at her. "You'd be too much trouble."

That hurt. But after hearing about the camping trip and the fact that they'd be riding horses, Olivia had to concede that she wouldn't add much. "Maybe I can find something to do until you leave," she answered, reluctantly envisioning cooking duty. It was obvious that John Paul hadn't checked with Luke, either. Well, it was Luke's fault that everything was so rushed.

"Forget it," the rancher said, shaking his head. "Hurry up. I need to rub down Star."

Olivia nodded and savored a few seconds of being still.

"Need some help?" He held out his arms.

"No, thanks." She was determined to do *something* on her own.

"Those muscles have had a workout," he warned.

"They're used to it. I have a personal fitness trainer."

Luke didn't move.

Neither did her legs. "I..."

Sympathy flickered in his eyes. "Hold on." He walked around to the other side of the horse and eased her foot out of the stirrup. "Slowly now."

"Absolutely," she said and began inching her leg over Star's back.

Her muscles screamed. Olivia gasped. Her supporting leg trembled noticeably and embarrassingly. She'd discovered a whole new muscle group that proved to be of no use at all.

The instant her foot touched the ground, she collapsed into a quivering mass of abused flesh. Or would have collapsed, if she'd been able to extricate her boot from the stirrup.

Star shifted and for one terrified moment, Olivia thought she was going to be dragged off to the corral, or wherever Star thought her next meal was coming from.

The next instant, Luke's arms closed around Olivia, holding her up as he worked her borrowed boot out of the stirrup.

Her relief at having both feet on the ground was tempered by the discovery that she couldn't stand upright without assistance.

"I'll never walk again," she moaned.

She heard Luke's chuckle rumble in his chest—a very solid chest. Thank goodness he still held her.

"Sure you will."

"Not in the foreseeable future." Olivia tried a few steps. "It feels like my legs are curved. That *is* temporary, isn't it?"

Luke's arm tightened briefly around her waist. "In a couple of days, all your curves will be back in the right places."

Olivia thought she heard a hint of a smile in his voice. She looked up. It *was* a smile. And...could that be a twinkle in his eyes?

She forgot the pain in her legs and smiled back. Luke's gaze fastened on her lips, and his head inched downward.

"Olivia, dear." John Paul hurried toward them. "The photographers have gone. Stop playing kissy-face with Mr. Chance and hustle yourself into the van."

Olivia had had quite enough of John Paul for one day. "We're leaving?" She was loath to abandon Luke's arms.

"I understood time was of the essence," John Paul said with a peevish look at Luke.

He lowered his arms. "I need to tend to the horses." He studied her as she walked a few steps. "Are you okay now?"

Olivia grimaced. "Not okay yet, but I think there's hope."

"Come *on* Olivia," John Paul urged. "If all goes well, you'll be back here in a few weeks."

"I'll be back here before then. Did you forget about the camping trip?" She cautiously moved toward the bunkhouse.

Fortunately she never unpacked everything at once. It was a long-ingrained habit left over from a childhood of quick hotel departures. As an adult, Olivia guessed that those hasty getaways had been to avoid paying the rent, but she'd never questioned her parents.

"Camping trip?" John Paul appeared genuinely puzzled.

"Bluebonnet's famous wilderness camping trip," she reminded him with a touch of sarcasm. "The one you told everyone I was going on?"

"Don't be absurd. You're not going anywhere except in that van. We want to catch the nine-o'clock flight to Houston. There's a midnight connection to New York."

"Wait a minute." Olivia stopped. "You mean this was just one of your publicity stunts?"

"And a very successful one. Now *do* get into the van. Your things are all packed."

She knew they were within earshot of Luke and couldn't help glancing back to see his reaction.

"So long," he said, tipping his hat and gathering the horses' reins. He turned away, but not before Olivia saw his lip curl in disgust at them.

Various emotions bombarded her. She was hurt that Luke could dismiss her so casually. But then why not? He barely knew her and probably thought she was no better than John Paul.

And if she left now, she wouldn't be. John Paul had crossed a moral line in the name of publicity, and Olivia wanted no part of it.

"You lied." She glared at him. "Exaggeration and hype are part of publicity, but outright lying is going too far."

"How high-minded you've become, darling."

Olivia felt her face burn. Although she should have known better, she'd been taken in. "I'm staying."

"No, you're not!" both men objected at the same time.

"But the boys think I'm staying. And they were in the pictures."

John Paul sighed with impatience. "Mr. Chance will tell them something, won't you?"

Luke's gaze flicked first over John Paul, then Olivia. "Yeah. Maybe the truth."

Suddenly a scream curdled the air.

It came from the bunkhouse. Olivia and John Paul stared. Luke ran. Seconds later, Simon cannoned out the side entrance.

"It's Angel!" Simon grabbed Luke's arm.

"The little one? Did he finally speak?"

"Oh, yeah." Simon heaved a breath as a slight figure holding a table knife appeared in the doorway. "It seems he's a *she*."

CHAPTER FIVE

"YOU MEAN TO TELL ME that's a *girl?*" Luke pointed at the defiant figure.

He—she—was dressed just like the others with baggy clothes, shaggy hair and a rebellious scowl.

Panting, Simon nodded.

"Olivia and I will say our farewells now. Mr. Chance," John Paul held out his hand. "It's been a pleasure—"

Luke ignored him. "How do you know?" he asked Simon, then closed his eyes. "Don't tell me. I'll take your word for it." Both men studied the girl.

She was the one who'd hung back from the others during the photo session. More than once, Olivia had been conscious of the dark eyes silently watching them.

John Paul tapped Luke on the arm in lieu of shaking his hand. "Say goodbye to Mr. Chance, Olivia."

"No." She couldn't just walk off and leave Luke. To her surprise, she'd discovered that at some point during her brief stay at Bluebonnet Ranch, Luke's opinion of her had become more important than John Paul's.

John Paul glared at her. "Mr. Chance is very busy and we have a plane connection to make."

"I'm staying." She gazed levelly at her producer. "You told everyone I was staying. And I'll bet you told Mr. Collingsworth I was staying, too." She would *not* let John Paul hurt her reputation with the new sponsor.

"Angel..." Luke took a step toward the girl.

"Keep away from me!" She crouched low and brandished the knife, looking more scared than threatening.

Luke stopped walking, but held his hands out, palms up. "No one's going to hurt you."

"You gonna make me stay in there with them?" She jerked her head in the direction of the bunkhouse. It was suspiciously quiet inside.

"No," Luke answered.

"Then what in Sam Hill are we going to do with her?" Simon asked.

Shaking his head, Luke sighed. It was a long, weary sigh, the kind made by someone who was tired but anticipated more work ahead. "We'll have to send her back."

"No! I don't want to go back! *He* promised." Angel lowered the knife.

Olivia wondered if "he" meant Mr. Collingsworth.

Luke wore a pained expression. "Honey, I'm sorry, but we're not set up for girls."

"What about *her?*" Angel pointed at Olivia.

Luke turned to Olivia in surprise. "She's not a girl."

"Now, wait a minute—"

The van's horn blared, cutting off Olivia. The *Lovers and Liars* crew was tired of waiting. "We were just leaving," John Paul announced, pushing Olivia toward the van.

"No!" Angel wailed, startling the already skittish horses.

Simon shouted a warning. Olivia stopped and John Paul plowed into her.

Luke's piercing whistle silenced the babble. "Whoa, people." He pointed. "Simon, take care of the horses. Angel, get your gear."

"I want to stay." Angel had changed from an angry, threatening youth to a tearful child. "Please?"

"Not without a chaperon." Luke shook his head firmly, but with obvious regret. He reached out and detained John Paul, who was trying to escape and take Olivia with him. "John Paul, how about doing me a favor and giving Angel a lift to the airport?"

"She... has a knife."

"Don't worry. They won't let her take it on the plane. I'll make a couple of calls and see if I can get her on your flight back to New York. You say you're connecting through Houston?"

For once, John Paul was speechless. Olivia took advantage. "That won't be necessary. I'm staying, so Angel can stay, too. We'll chaperon each other."

John Paul looked as though he wanted to strangle someone. "You might want to rethink your decision, dear."

It was the perfect solution as far as Olivia was concerned. Angel could remain, and John Paul would learn to think twice before volunteering the cast of *Lovers and Liars* for personal appearances without checking their schedules first.

"You told the world I was staying. You told *Bettina* I was staying." Olivia accompanied the emphasis with a significant look that said, *Don't you think she'll verify that I'm still here?*

John Paul tilted his bearded chin. "And now I'll tell the world you had prior commitments—like taping some scenes?"

"What scenes?" Olivia asked. "You won't start this new story line for a couple of weeks—you'll be building sets."

"Rehearsals." He narrowed his eyes. "I can't be responsible for what happens if you don't show up for rehearsals."

"That sounds like a threat." Olivia turned to Luke and Angel. "Didn't that sound like a threat to you?"

Luke cleared his throat. "I'm not set up for females this go-round," he said, sidestepping an answer to her question. "If y'all will take Angel, I'd appreciate it."

Angel shrieked and collapsed in a sobbing heap.

The two men, one a decisive rancher, the other a shrewd producer, both looked at Olivia with identical expressions of helpless dismay.

How could they be fooled by such overwrought dramatics? Olivia rolled her eyes, then took charge. "John Paul, please get my things from the van. I'll need to return Tom's boots to him. Luke, since we can't stay in the bunkhouse, Angel and I will just move up to the ranch house." She bestowed her sweetest smile on the dumbfounded men and went to Angel.

"You're going to st-stay?" The girl hiccuped the last word.

Olivia joined her on the step. "Of course I am. In fact, I'll sit right here while you go pack your things." Provided, of course, her aching legs cooperated.

Angel scrubbed her cheeks and stood. Eyeing Luke and John Paul, she reached down and handed Olivia the knife. "I don't trust the pale one."

"Neither do I, Angel. Neither do I."

As soon as the girl disappeared inside, John Paul marched over. "Olivia, this is impossible. I insist you come at once. We're already late, and I hold you fully responsible."

Olivia frowned and brandished the knife as she'd seen Angel do. John Paul skidded to a halt. Hey, it worked!

Extending the knife in one hand, Olivia tugged off her boots with the other. She tossed them at John Paul.

Luke watched silently for a moment, then sauntered to the van, withdrew Olivia's suitcase and brought it to her. "I'm unarmed," he murmured.

Olivia smothered a smile.

"Well, I never!" John Paul huffed and puffed a couple of times, then stomped over to the van. "You'll be hearing from me!" He turned and climbed inside.

Behind his back, Olivia waggled her fingers at the crew. The driver gave her a thumbs-up.

"He's a weasel," the returning Angel said. They watched the van drive off.

"Yes, but he's a talented weasel, or I wouldn't put up with him." Olivia hesitated, then handed her the knife, hoping Angel would see that she trusted her.

And hoping Angel *wouldn't* see her holding her breath.

As she took her running shoes out of her suitcase, Olivia watched Angel voluntarily surrender the table knife to Luke. "I don't need this anymore."

"No, you don't," Luke replied. "I'm glad you realized that."

Olivia exhaled. She tied her shoes and straightened, colliding with Luke's searching gaze. It plumbed straight through to her soul and took her measure.

Time stopped as Olivia and Luke communicated on some deep, intimate level only they could hear.

Why are you doing this? he seemed to be asking.

To help.

Why? Why here?

Because you need me.

I got along fine without you for years.

But you need me now.

You have no idea what you're getting into.

I'm stronger than you think.

Luke's eyes narrowed, and he nodded infinitesimally. *You'll have to be.*

From that moment on, Olivia knew their relationship had changed. She was no longer playing a part—she was living one. She'd abandoned her world and entered Luke's. Could she meet the challenge?

Luke reached down and lifted her suitcase. "Welcome to Bluebonnet Ranch, ladies. Can I interest you in some barbecue?"

The instant Olivia entered the ranch house, all thoughts of food fled.

The house itself wasn't large. Luke had been telling the truth when he'd said he wasn't equipped to handle visitors.

They walked into a den with a stone fireplace taking up one wall. On the opposite wall, Olivia caught a glimpse of a room that appeared to be an office. The den flowed into a modest dining area. The kitchen, though, was restaurant-size. Looking around, Olivia saw that it was connected to the chow house, where she and the crew had eaten.

There were only two bedrooms. One was the master suite and obviously Luke's. The other, he tersely informed them, was used by his housekeeper during her weekly visits.

But it was the master bathroom that captured Olivia's attention. She ignored the serviceable shower and headed for the charming claw-foot tub, which sat under a skylight.

A bathtub, a bathtub! her muscles sang. Or were they crying?

"This is unexpected," she commented, turning to him.

Luke stuck his hands into the back pockets of his jeans. "It was a gift."

Olivia waited, but he didn't elaborate. "It's gorgeous."

He nodded. "Had a devil of a time installing it. I don't use it much."

"Why not?" Standing near the edge of the tub and looking upward, Olivia could see the setting sun's oranges and golds streak the sky. And when it was dark, she knew stars would twinkle there.

"A shower's faster."

Olivia wasn't interested in fast. Her aching muscles craved a long soak in the starlight. No barbecue for her.

Luke opened a cabinet. "Clean linens in here. I wasn't expecting overnight guests." He pulled out sheets and towels and handed them to Angel. "Looks like you're bunking in the housekeeper's room."

He pulled out another set of sheets and towels, which he handed to Olivia. "And you can have my room."

"Where will you be?" she asked.

Luke shot Olivia a dark look. "With Simon and the boys. You ladies will have the house to yourselves."

He and Angel disappeared through the door.

Just a few more minutes, Olivia promised her whimpering muscles and went to help Angel make her bed.

"When you're settled, c'mon around to the kitchen and have some supper," Luke said. "I'm going to see how the others are doing." He nodded and left.

Olivia and Angel worked in silence. Although there were a lot of questions Olivia wanted to ask the girl, she kept quiet. Time enough for confidences later, when Angel felt more comfortable around her.

"He's a nice man," Angel said suddenly. "My cousin came here last summer. Now it's all he talks about. After my uncle died, my cousin was supposed to be the head of the family, but all he did was hang out with his friends. My aunt would cry." Angel slowly smoothed the wrinkles from the sheet.

"I'm sorry," Olivia said, feeling at a loss to know what to say.

"No, it's okay now." Angel's face brightened. "He... he was arrested, but instead of going to jail, he came here. And now everything's different. He has a job after school, and he studies all the time. He says..." Angel's voice lowered to an awed whisper. "He says that if his grades are good and he graduates from high school, Mr. Luke will give him a scholarship. For *college.*"

Olivia looked at Angel's glowing face and felt her heart give a little blip. There was nothing in the brochures about scholarships. Olivia wondered if anyone knew about it.

"I wanted that for me," Angel continued. "But my cousin, he says I can't come here. Only boys."

"So you pretended to be a boy."

Angel finished tucking in the sheet. "Yes." She chewed her lip. "Do you think if I do good, Mr. Luke will give me a scholarship?"

Olivia had no idea what Luke's arrangement was with the youths he brought here. How could he afford to give scholarships to them all? Or was that what Mr. Collingsworth did? *Mr. Collingsworth.* No telling what his reaction would be when he discovered Angel's duplicity. "I..."

Angel regarded her intently. Olivia had been about to say that she didn't know anything about the scholarships, but the desperate hope in Angel's face stopped her. "I never went to college," she replied, instead.

"No? Well, you do good here," Angel told her, "and maybe Mr. Luke will give you a scholarship, too."

"Maybe." Olivia smiled. "Say, I'm not very hungry, but I can vouch for the barbecue. Why don't you go on to the chow house, and I'll catch up with you later?"

As Angel left the bedroom, Olivia found herself thinking that if Luke couldn't afford another scholarship, she knew of a certain New York producer whose arm she could twist.

But for now, the glorious tub was calling her.

On her way back to the bathroom, Olivia peeked into the pantry, trying to avoid being spotted by anyone. She was looking for candles; she knew anyone this far from civilization would have candles on hand for power failures. And relaxing, shadowy baths.

They were almost too easy to find. Boxes of white emergency candles were stacked on a back shelf along with hurricane lamps, batteries, flashlights, matches, a radio and other assorted supplies.

Her thighs burned as she crept back to the bedroom, carrying two hurricane lamps and the candles. She poured a liberal amount of atrociously expensive bath gel into the tub and turned on the tap. As the tub filled, Olivia lighted the lamps and the candles, turned out the light and stripped off her clothes.

Two large patches of skin on her inner thighs were rubbed raw by her jeans. The sores stung in the soapy water, but easing herself into the tub, Olivia decided the momentary pain was worth it.

She'd been so eager to immerse herself in the hot water, she'd forgotten to pin up her shoulder-length hair. After a day under a hat, it needed to be washed, anyway, so she leaned back and forgot about it.

It was blessedly quiet, except for the distant murmur of voices from the chow house. Through the skylight, she watched the sunset's pinks and oranges darken to lavenders and purples. The evening stars winked as the night sky navied.

Olivia was reminded of time passing only because the water cooled. She drew more hot water until the bubbles were just below the rim of the tub. Even sitting up to reach the faucet hurt. How could she ever leave the tub?

Would she ever be able to move again?

She made a face. Not only was she going to have to move again, she was going to have to get back on a horse—and soon. At the moment, nothing was less appealing.

But at the moment, she ought to be on her way back to New York.

She'd made the morally right choice in staying at Bluebonnet Ranch, hadn't she? It wasn't like her to make a fuss about anything. She'd carefully established a professional reputation for being dependable and cooperative. She had created and sustained a character for more than a decade.

And that character might, *might,* be headed for a coma.

Olivia shifted, sending a tiny wave of bubbles perilously near the edge. Did John Paul truly think Mr. Collingsworth wouldn't hear the publicity about Olivia volunteering to work at the ranch and then wonder when she didn't show up?

Thinking of the thwarted John Paul, she smiled, finding she could still do so without pain. How many other times had she or the rest of the cast been victims of his publicity hype? How many fans had she unknowingly disappointed or hurt? This was a good cause for her to support. Yes, she was right to stay.

The water had cooled again. She was going to have to sit up if she wanted to draw more. Maybe if she kneaded her legs, it would soothe the muscles.

Olivia shifted and groaned.

"You okay?"

She screamed. Twice. Once from being startled and again from the sudden tensing of her mistreated muscles.

And that was even before she'd registered the voice as belonging to Luke.

She sank farther below the bubble line. "*What* are you doing in here?"

"I came to see if you were okay." Luke carefully moved one of the hurricane lamps aside and leaned against the sink.

"Can't you see if I'm okay," she said with emphasis, "from *outside* the door?"

"I heard all the moaning and thought you and Angel were killing each other." He smiled without a trace of self-consciousness, looking nothing like a man who thought he was interrupting a murder. Looking very much at home, in fact.

Was he just going to stand there? "Angel went to eat."

"Didn't see her."

"Well, I *guarantee* she's not in here!" Olivia became more and more aware of the crackling pops as her bubble cover thinned. A gap formed near her knee. She didn't dare move.

And Luke apparently didn't plan to.

The candlelight threw shadows into the corners of the bathroom and, Olivia hoped, onto the tub, as well.

"Uh, Luke?"

"Hmm?" He slowly shifted his gaze from the ever-widening gap to her face.

Olivia caught her breath.

This was no aw-shucks cowboy struck dumb by her sophisticated presence. His smile was more mysterious than the Mona Lisa. Full of secrets and memories.

Pleasant memories.

His eyebrow arched the slightest fraction, as if inviting her to create more memories with him.

He wasn't wearing his hat, she noticed suddenly, admiring how his thick brown hair gleamed in the candlelight.

He looked younger without his hat.

And more attractive.

And infinitely more dangerous to her peace of mind.

She remembered his kiss—did she *ever* remember it. His gaze dropped to her mouth. He remembered it, too.

Her lips tingled. Water lapped in time with her quickened breathing. Her heart—the only muscle that wasn't sore—thumped.

The candles flickered. Olivia's blanket of bubbles grew more threadbare.

"Want me to scrub your back?"

"No." She cleared her throat.

"I was afraid of that." He sighed. "I suppose you're raw in a couple of spots."

More than a couple, but she nodded.

"I brought some ointment and bandages."

"Thank you." Ever conscious of her disappearing bubbles, Olivia added, "You can leave them on the dresser in the bedroom."

"I did."

Still, he stood there, the corners of his mouth quivering. "I'll be on my way as soon as I pack a few of my things."

"Fine." *Leave!*

Opening the medicine cabinet, he removed a razor and an old-fashioned shaving mug. "I suppose there's no reason for me to stay in here, then."

"None whatsoever," she said primly.

"Especially since the mirror gives me such a good view."

Olivia's gaze flew to the mirror over the sink, which reflected the bedroom.

Luke grinned. "You'll want to get out of the tub, anyway. Your bubbles are nearly gone."

Olivia could feel a blush beginning at her toes and traveling all the way up her body. She squeaked and groped for the washcloth. "Luke! Shut the door!"

He was already on his way out, hand on the knob. He turned and looked back at her.

"Maybe I will." He rattled the knob, then winked. "And maybe I won't."

CHAPTER SIX

HE DIDN'T SHUT THE DOOR.

Olivia's gaze remained riveted to the mirror. Luke whistled as he stuffed clothes into a duffel bag and left within moments.

And then proceeded to ignore her for the next two days. Well, not completely. No, she was instructed along with Angel and the boys in how to care for a horse. Star, in Olivia's case.

She patted the even-tempered horse she'd just attempted to saddle. "Good Star. If you hold still while I fasten this thingie, I'll let you have a squirt of Moon Shadows."

Star snorted, and Olivia laughed. "You'd prefer food? Just between us, you could stand to cut back a little. You're looking a mite tubby."

Olivia rubbed her own midsection. She should cut back herself. The ranch food was hearty and plentiful. In other words, cholesterol-laden, teenage-boy-size portions. And those fresh cinnamon rolls every morning...

Star shifted, something she did a lot. Olivia had trained herself not to jump every time the horse twitched. She reached out now to stroke Star's neck where her black mane spilled over the side of her neck. She held a lock of her own dark brown hair next to

Star's. Her silky tresses and Star's coarse hair were almost a perfect match.

"Wow, look at those split ends, girl. You could stand a trim, or at least a hot oil treatment." Olivia leaned close and whispered in the horse's ear. "And we both know they've got plenty of oil in the kitchen."

A week ago, she'd been in New York, and if anyone had told her she was about to go to Texas and make friends with a horse, she would've crossed them off her *A* list.

A week ago, she'd had a manicure.

A week ago, she'd been contentedly employed. Today, she wasn't sure she even still had a job. She'd checked with Tony, her agent, daily, and so far, John Paul hadn't fired her. Olivia had no doubt her little rebellion would have consequences, but she hoped John Paul would forgive and forget when he saw all the positive publicity. But in case he didn't, Tony was discreetly spreading the word that Olivia Faraday's contract was up for renewal, and she *might* be interested in something else.

In the meantime, no news was good news.

"Tighten the cinch."

Olivia jumped. She hadn't heard Luke approach. "Won't that hurt the horse?"

"No," he said, tugging on the saddle blanket. "But it'll hurt you if you fall off the horse because the saddle turns."

Olivia watched as Luke demonstrated how he wanted her to saddle Star.

His manner was impersonal. He treated Olivia the same as he treated everyone. She saw nothing of the intriguing rancher who had interrupted her bath.

Olivia could almost think of that night without cringing. As soon as the screen door had slammed behind Luke, Olivia was out of the water, amazed she could move so quickly. She'd spent the next several minutes dripping in a towel and peering at the bathtub from his vantage points.

With relief, she'd concluded that between the shadows and the bubbles, he hadn't seen more than her head. The whole incident could be chalked up to harmless teasing. After all, she was the one who'd left the bedroom and bathroom doors wide open.

But his expression hadn't been teasing. And it was the frank and unapologetic desire she'd seen in his eyes that she couldn't forget, even though there was no trace of it now.

"Now let's see you do it," he directed, removing the saddle and handing it to her.

Olivia staggered, then tossed the whole thing back onto Star. Poor Star. She bore Olivia's inexperience with a stoicism Olivia appreciated.

Tightening the cinch, she looked to Luke for approval. He made a minor adjustment, then nodded, his expression cool and polite. "You and Angel can muck out the stalls this evening."

"Muck out the stalls? I don't like the sound of 'muck.'"

"Most people don't like the smell of muck," Luke replied and handed her a rake. "Fresh straw is over there." He pointed and checked his watch. "Better hurry, or you won't have time to clean up before supper."

Ah, that was the plan, she thought. Get Olivia good and dirty and pay a visit when she's soaking in the tub. Did he think she wouldn't shut the door this time?

"Is this really necessary?" she asked. "We're leaving on the camping trip in a couple of days."

His gaze flicked over her shoulder. Olivia heard a raspy sound that told her Angel was already mucking.

Angel's eagerness significantly weakened Olivia's bargaining position. Olivia admired the girl's single-minded pursuit of a scholarship, but was exasperated by her uncomplaining subservience.

"Everybody is expected to pull his own weight around here—even skinny gals like you."

"Luke."

He'd already started to walk off, automatically assuming she'd leap to obey. He turned back, eyebrow raised.

"Drop the hick routine, okay?"

"I don't know what you mean," he said innocently.

Olivia had used his ranch house office to phone Tony every day. Her agent invariably placed her on hold, and she had ample time to study the certificates, plaques and framed photographs crowding the walls. Civic awards from the governors of two states, certificates of appreciation, plaques proclaiming him a significant contributor to several universities—all were there for her to read.

But it was the photographs that astonished Olivia. He and Mr. Collingsworth were featured in several, but there were others of Luke with the governor of New York, Luke with a university chancellor, Luke with a society maven. He was dressed like a successful businessman in all of them.

Which explained the two pricy-label suits she'd shoved aside in his closet when she'd hung up her clothes. And the pair of soft-leather Italian shoes that wouldn't stand up to a day of his normal routine here at Bluebonnet.

No, Luke might be a rancher, but he was also on the board of directors of the Bluebonnet Foundation. Every March they held the famous Bluebonnet Ball. Olivia had heard of it, of course, but hadn't connected it to Luke until her agent had filled her in.

With a glance toward the industrious Angel, Olivia took Luke's elbow and stepped outside the stables. "I have just one word to say to you." She paused for emphasis. "Armani."

"Ar-who?"

Hands on her hips, Olivia shook her head. "Don't play dumb with me, cowboy. Armani designed those suits in your closet."

Luke squinted off into the distance. "I see you've made yourself at home."

"I didn't need to read the label. *I* can't afford an Armani suit, but Diana D'Angelo wears them sometimes."

"She probably looks real good in them."

"You probably do, too."

He grinned and glanced down at her. "That's what Mrs. Collingsworth thought."

"She has good taste."

He looked impatient. "Is that all that's bothering you?"

"It wasn't *bothering* me," Olivia started to explain. "I just didn't know who you were until I talked with my agent yesterday."

Luke crossed his arms over his chest. "You've got your agent investigating me?"

Olivia opened, then closed her mouth. This conversation was supposed to proceed along entirely different lines resulting in Olivia's being relieved of some of the grub work she'd been assigned. "I didn't have to. I read your walls. Besides, my agent has better things to do. One of those things is to follow my publicity. There's a story about you in one of the fan magazines that sent reporters out here to take pictures."

His eyes widened. "How'd they find out about me?"

"My guess is the Collingsworths. They were interviewed, too."

Luke removed his hat and ran a hand through his hair. "They told me to expect media attention," he said, staring at his hat brim. "I just didn't figure..."

He glanced up, piercing her with a bright blue gaze. "I just didn't figure on you."

Now how was she supposed to take that? She decided to play it casual. "And I didn't figure on you. I certainly didn't figure on *mucking* out any stables." She smiled, hoping she seemed a sweet and reasonable good sport. "I think I have the flavor of ranch life now."

"Is *this*—" he gestured with his hat at the ranch house and bluebonnet-adorned bunkhouse "—what you think ranch life is?"

A trick question. If she answered yes, she was obviously going to be shown differently. There were probably all sorts of icky chores he could find for her to do. If she said no, she'd probably be faced with all sorts of icky chores, anyway. A no-win situation. "I'm sure there's a lot to running a ranch that I don't know about. However, with all due respect and admiration, I don't feel a burning desire to experience life as a ranch hand."

"Then you shouldn't have volunteered."

The ungrateful so-and-so. "You *know* I didn't volunteer."

Luke clamped the hat back on his head. "Lady, you wanted to stay so bad you held a knife on me."

"I..." She had, hadn't she? "I can explain that."

"Tell me all about it *after* you finish in the stables." He clasped her shoulders, turned her around and escorted her to the abandoned rake.

"But—"

"Supper's in an hour. We're gonna have grits and fried ham tonight."

Grits? *Fried* ham? Her arteries clogged at the thought. "If it wouldn't be too much trouble, could the cook—after he's finished with the grits and all—perhaps grill a piece of fish? A little green side salad and lemon would be nice, too. Nothing as fancy or complicated as...grits."

"It's grits or nothing. And if I were you, I wouldn't want to be last. Grits stick to the bottom of the pot, and truth to tell, they aren't at their best then."

"Grits don't have a best at all," she mumbled.

"What's that?"

Olivia smiled. "I said I'll be right along as soon as I finish the rest of these stalls."

Luke smiled back.

Olivia wondered what it would cost to bribe a grocery delivery boy to drive from Austin.

But maybe Luke would reward her efforts of the past several days and let her have her fish and salad.

Olivia raked until her hands blistered. The dust and the straw irritated her nose, but she continued, enduring the prickles and the general yuckiness of her chore until she felt the stable had been mucked enough.

Angel had finished earlier. She worked faster, and in fairness, Olivia had sent her on in to supper.

But enough was enough. "'Bye, Star," she said to her equine friend and trudged up to the ranch house.

Sounds from the chow house drifted on the balmy evening air. The boys nearly had the whole place to themselves, just as they did the bunkhouse. Simon had told her that the other ranch hands and their families were housed in the cluster of buildings visible in the distance. The bunkhouse was only used for extra workers.

Since it was spring, the hands were riding the range looking for new calves, branding and counting. Other than Simon, who was the foreman, the cook and Mrs. Royer, the housekeeper, who came to the ranch once a week, Olivia hadn't met any other ranch employees.

"All finished?" a deep voice asked. Luke sat on the edge of the porch.

Olivia nearly tripped up the step to the ranch house. "Quit sneaking up on me!"

"I saw you leave the stables. Been waiting here a full minute." He appeared unruffled.

"There's a big difference between waiting out in the open and lurking in the shadows," she grumbled.

"You're from the big city. You ought to be experienced at ferreting out shadow lurkers."

She made a face. "What did you want, anyway?"

"Angel's been back awhile. I wanted to see if you were about finished." He pushed himself off the porch.

"More than finished. I can now add mucking out a stable to my body of knowledge."

"Let's take a look." He loped toward the stables.

"*What?* You're going to inspect?" she called after him.

"Yep."

Olivia drew a deep breath. Then another. She didn't care what he thought of the condition of the stables. She wasn't one of his boys. And she wasn't a ranch hand. She wasn't getting paid to do this.

Olivia examined her stinging hands. There wasn't enough money around to pay her to muck out the stables again. Long ago, she'd vowed not to degrade herself to get acting work. Although this wasn't strictly for her job, it was close enough.

Besides, look at that manicure. Luke obviously had no idea how much it cost for a set of acrylic nails these days. And next time, the manicurist would have to start from scratch.

But had she complained? No. Had she asked for special treatment? Except for an extremely reasonable request for fish tonight, no.

Had Luke expressed any gratitude at all?

No.

She wanted a bath and she wanted it now.

Olivia actually got as far as the top step before turning around and jogging after Luke. He was bound to be impressed with their work in the stables and Olivia wasn't averse to soaking up a little praise before soaking in a bath.

"It stinks in here." He stood in the doorway, hands on his hips.

"News flash, Luke. Your horses aren't potty-trained."

"If you'd done your job properly, the stable wouldn't smell."

Poor man. Over the years, his nose must have become desensitized. "I was going to suggest some room fresheners liberally placed throughout, say one per stall? Maybe in a pine scent?"

Luke ignored her and walked from stall to stall, poking at straw with his boot. "You didn't rake these out completely, did you?"

"I raked out all the pertinent parts."

He shot her a disgusted look and pointed to the heap she and Angel had left outside. "Why didn't you haul that away?"

Haul? "And put it where?" Olivia stormed the length of the stalls. "You didn't say anything about hauling. I distinctly heard mucking."

"Hauling is part of mucking."

"How am I supposed to know that? I've never been to a ranch. The only mucking I've ever seen is the clowns who follow the Clydesdales in the St. Patrick's Day parade."

This earned her a smile. A small one. "I should have been more specific," he admitted. "You'll need to rake out *all* the old straw and spread new."

"Next time, I'll know." Of course, there wasn't going to be a next time.

"*This* time." Luke walked over to the wall where the rakes, bridles and assorted bits of leather and metal hung. He chose a lethal-looking pitchfork and handed it to her.

Olivia gazed at him in disbelief. "You don't expect me to do this right now?"

He nodded.

"By myself?" There were eight stalls on a side. It would take hours.

"Somebody's got to do it."

"Well, it can be *somebody* else!" She slammed the pitchfork against the wall, whirled around and stalked out.

That was it. No more. She'd had it.

She'd mucked, raked, cleaned, combed and polished.

She'd overcome her terror of horses and ridden herself raw, lugged saddles and then learned to care for and feed her horse. While she and Star would never be best friends, they were now on a first-name basis.

"Olivia!"

That ingrate! She'd saved his skin. John Paul's, too. Olivia expanded her anger to include the producer. If she hadn't stayed at Bluebonnet, she had no doubt that Bettina would have trumpeted that fact far and wide. Olivia would have looked bad. John Paul, even though he'd somehow wiggle out of it, would have looked bad. The show would have looked bad. Mr. Collingsworth would have been angry.

"Come back here!"

And as for Luke... Angel was smart and determined and desperate. By sending her back, even for a very good reason, he was opening himself up to charges of discrimination. Bettina, with an obvious eye on a spot on network news, was aching to sink her teeth into a real meaty story.

Was Olivia the only one concerned about these possibilities?

Luke grabbed her arm. "Where are you going?"

She looked pointedly at his hand. "I am going to take a bath. Then I am going to eat my dinner."

"What about the stables?"

Olivia snatched her arm out of his grasp. "What about them?"

"They're your responsibility."

"And Angel's," Olivia reminded him.

"You told her she could leave."

"My mistake." Olivia tried to push past him.

"Whoa, there."

"No more cowboy talk!" she snarled.

"Okay." He stared down at her. "What do you intend to do about the stables?"

"Nothing."

"I don't tolerate this kind of attitude from the kids in the program, and I won't tolerate it from you."

Olivia's jaw dropped. The nerve! The gall! The conceit! "I am *not* one of your inner-city refugees!"

"Aren't you?"

"No!"

Luke slid his hands into his back pockets. "I don't mean you live on the streets or run with a gang, but I figured you were avoiding something back in New York."

"John Paul and his sleazy publicity tactics."

"Is that all?"

"That's all I'm going to discuss with you." She started up the stairs.

"Whatever the reason, you stayed. You accepted the responsibility."

Olivia dropped her head, sighing deeply. Apparently they were going to hash out their differences before she could take a bath and eat.

"I stayed as a chaperon for Angel. Therefore, it's reasonable to expect me to participate in the routine and to learn to ride and care for the horse. But it is not reasonable to expect me to clean out the stables by myself!"

He propped a booted foot on the first step. "We rotate chores. It was your turn."

"I don't think so." She smiled, but without mirth. "It doesn't take a mathematical genius to see that there are more boys than there are days we'll be here."

"If I'd put you in the kitchen helping the cook, you would have accused me of stereotyping you."

"I wouldn't have had to once you'd tasted my cooking." Although privately, she thought she could do at least as well as his current cook.

"The problem is that a lot of chores need a good strong back. It's hard work running a ranch."

"What do you do for slaves when we're not here?"

That was the wrong thing to say. Olivia braced herself for the explosion.

Surprisingly a corner of Luke's mouth tilted. "Part of the success of our program is that the kids know they're doing real work, not invented work." He pointed back to the stables. "I wouldn't keep those horses if it weren't for the boys coming each summer."

"So who cares for them during the fall and winter?"

"Some are loaners from other ranchers. For the rest, I hire local school kids, either the sons and daughters of my own employees or neighbors' kids. The money goes into a special education fund that they have access to when they graduate from high school."

"Sounds very practical. And expensive."

"It is."

Olivia reluctantly concluded that she owed Luke an apology. "I'm sorry about the slave remark. I'm really tired."

She smiled a no-hard-feelings smile and continued up the stairs.

"You forgot about the stables." Luke's voice was firm and implaccable.

And unbelievable.

Olivia turned and looked down at him. He stood at the bottom of the steps, hands on his hips, obviously prepared to argue all night.

Olivia wasn't. "I didn't forget," she said in a controlled tone. "I've done all I can tonight. Each stall was cleaned even though it wasn't up to your standards. The horses will survive, but I might not—unless I immerse myself in hot water immediately."

"Would you want to sleep on soiled bedding?"

Olivia exhaled, her eyes squeezed shut. "No." What now? Would he make her sleep in the stables?

"We all work hard. I don't ask anyone to do anything I don't do myself. If you get any special treatment, discipline will be shot."

"Why *shouldn't* I be entitled to special treatment?" Olivia could feel her anger build. She wanted to remain in control, but it was becoming very difficult in the face of this extremely stubborn cowboy. "I'm a volunteer. An actress. One of my *chores,* if you will, was to bring you publicity. And I have. A lot of it."

"You wanted to be a real participant. Not window dressing."

Olivia's breath hissed between her teeth. "Nobody is going to come and photograph the stables!" She marched inside.

Luke followed. "I should've known you couldn't handle it."

Olivia smirked. "Is this where I'm supposed to get mad and vow to prove to you otherwise?"

"It's worked before." He looked very sure of himself.

"Not this time." She tilted her chin. "I quit."

CHAPTER SEVEN

"YOU WON'T QUIT." Luke was irritatingly sure of himself. "You're forgetting Angel."

"What about her?"

"If you leave, she'll have to leave, too."

"Tough."

His eyes narrowed. "You don't mean it." But doubt had crept into his tone.

Olivia crossed her arms over her chest. "Angel doesn't like ranch life any more than I do."

Luke blinked. "Then why is she here?"

Certainly not from a burning desire to clean up after animals that aren't housebroken. "Because you gave her cousin a scholarship and she wants one, too."

He drew his brows together. "What's her cousin's name?"

"*I* don't know." Olivia sighed. If he had to ask, then that meant he'd given out more than one scholarship. "You really are a saint, aren't you?" She gazed up at the tall rancher in unwilling admiration.

"I beg your pardon?"

Olivia threw up her hands. "I can't compete with saints. In spite of it all, I'm going to come out looking like the bad guy." She headed for the bedroom without caring if he followed or not.

But he did follow. "You *are* tired," Luke said from the doorway. He raised one arm to grasp the top of the doorjamb and hooked the thumb of his other hand on the waist of his jeans.

Olivia jerked open the closet door and grabbed her robe off the hanger. "Look, anybody as determined as Angel deserves a chance at college. I'm *not* abandoning her, but I can do her more good as a working actress than as a fake ranch hand."

Luke studied her for several moments. "Scholarships only go to those who complete the Bluebonnet program."

"I *knew* it." Olivia flung the robe at the bed. "I knew you were going to make me the bad guy. I can see it now." She gestured imaginary headlines. "Soap Queen Pops Girl's Dream Bubble. And then the interview with Lucas Chance, philanthropist-rancher." She lowered her voice. "I'm sorry, but scholarships only go to those who complete the Bluebonnet program. When Miss Faraday backed out, there was no one to chaperon Angel. I had no choice."

"Well, if you leave, I won't." He sounded so reasonable, so logical and so infuriatingly male.

"Oh, no, you don't." Olivia glared at him. "I'll see that Angel gets enough money for college if I have to print it myself!"

She snatched the robe off the bed and proceeded to the bathroom. Just before she closed the door, she called to him with excruciating politeness, "Will you please arrange for a cab to pick me up tomorrow morning?"

Hearing no acknowledgment, she peered out the door. Had he left?

No, a pensive Luke still lounged in the doorway.

Hadn't anyone ever stood up to him before? Or hadn't a *woman* stood up to him before?

Olivia guessed that he was revising his entire impression of her. Probably of all womankind.

In fact, Olivia would go as far as to say that Lucas Chance was that species of man who had never encountered much resistance from women. Certainly not from her. She'd been dazzled by the Lucas Chance mystique. That could be the only explanation for her recent behavior.

After this evening, she was no longer dazzled. Yes, he was noble. No, John Paul was not. But John Paul had a direct effect on her standard of living and Luke didn't. It was time she remembered the financial facts of life.

Luke shifted, dropping his arm. Ah, he was going to make a decree.

"You serious about leaving?"

Not much of a decree. "Yes."

"Okay."

And he left. Just walked off. His boots sounded all the way across the wooden floor. Rhythmically. Unhesitatingly. Stopping only when he opened the screen door and allowed it to bang. Olivia couldn't even attribute an angry slam to the sound. Luke had merely opened the door and allowed it to close on its own.

She stared after him. Was it too much to hope for a little begging and groveling?

Apparently. Okay, one might say she was being difficult, but these were difficult times. She refused to be a doormat, and if standing up for herself meant being difficult, then so be it.

Still, disappointment shot through her, to her disgust. What was the matter with her? She'd wanted her own way. She'd gotten her own way—with minimum fuss.

But she really didn't want her own way. She wanted begging and groveling. She wanted special attention.

From Luke.

It was a long time later when she emerged from the tub, donned a delicate peach nightgown and began to blow-dry her hair. She'd been so dirty she'd showered first, then soaked in soothing bubbles. The bath gel was running out, so it was time to go home. She didn't think she could survive ranch life without bubbles.

She switched off the blow-dryer and flipped back her hair. Looking good, she thought, studying her reflection in the small mirror over the bureau. Her hair always responded to a rest from the gooey sprays and constant combing that Diana's sophisticated mane required.

There was a tap on the bedroom door. "Angel?" she called. "Is that you?"

"She's down at the stables with the boys," came Luke's smooth drawl. "They're polishing the tack and feeding the horses." *As you should be,* his tone implied.

Luke. Olivia grabbed her satin robe and tightened the sash.

"I brought you some supper," he said when she opened the door. "Cook was cleaning up."

Oh, boy, cold grits. Olivia would have declined, but recognized that this was a peace offering. She remembered the time Diana dated a diplomat and he whisked her off to an exotic clime where she was served sheep's eyes at a royal dinner.

"Why, thank you," Olivia said in a sugary tone, accompanied by the dazzling smile Diana had used to distract the royal prince from the fact that she wasn't eating.

Luke, smiling with lazy amusement, gestured for her to precede him into the dining room. "Table for one?"

The chow house's nondescript white china managed to look elegant sitting on the woven place mat that graced the dining table. This was real Southwestern-style and not the faux stuff New York had gone crazy about a couple of years back.

"Is that green I see? An actual vegetable?" She sat and pointed to a small bowl next to the plate. On the plate resided a black-and-pink piece of something. Never mind.

"Baby lettuce from the kitchen garden," Luke said. "Ran out of grits."

"What a pity." She glanced up to see an almost-smile cross his face. "But the lettuce more than makes up for the disappointment."

"I thought it might. By the way, we didn't have any fish in the freezer."

"It looks like you managed filet of sole, anyway." She gestured to the plate. "I do hope the cook has another pair of shoes."

His face creased into a grin. "Wait'll you see this." He disappeared into the kitchen and returned with a plate and a cream pitcher.

Olivia's eyes zeroed in on the telltale red and white. "Strawberry shortcake! Oh, I shouldn't."

"Fresh-picked strawberries and—" he held up the cream pitcher "—you'll never eat anything like this in New York."

Olivia's mouth watered. "It's full of fat."

"That's why it tastes good." He waved the shortcake under her nose and placed it and the cream well within reach.

Olivia swallowed. "I suppose I can indulge if I forego the—" she tried to identify the object on her plate "—ham?"

"If you insist," he said, whisking away the plate and leaving the room before she could change her mind. Not that she would.

Once in the kitchen, she heard him call, "Travis! Come here, boy. Looks like you get supper, after all."

Luke returned to a stone-faced Olivia. Her teeth hurt from clenching them. "I was depriving the stable dog of his supper?"

"Travis didn't mind sharing." Grinning, Luke pulled out a chair and straddled it.

She hated it when men sat that way. It was so uncouth.

Luke crossed his arms over the chair back and leaned his chin on them, watching as she bit into the lettuce.

He'd remembered her request for lemon and had included a wedge on the side, but Olivia didn't bother with it once she sampled the velvety leaves. A fresh, mild taste filled her mouth, cleansing it of the memory of heavy fried foods and barbecue. "This is wonderful. You all ought to eat more fresh vegetables. It's much healthier."

"If we ate as much rabbit food as you, we'd be hungry most of the time."

Olivia didn't reply. She was frequently hungry. The camera was worse than scales. "If *you* go on a strawberry-shortcake binge, it's between you and your jeans. I've got the camera to worry about."

"You don't have anything to worry about." He tilted his head to one side, his gaze sweeping her face. "You're very lovely."

She smiled perfunctorily. "Thanks."

"I see you've heard that before. What I meant," he said, touching her chin until she met his eyes, "is that you have a strong face. You've got those high cheekbones like my mother."

Like his.

"She was always a handsome woman, even when she wasn't young anymore. She never wore much makeup." He shrugged. "When you're not wearing your Diana face, you remind me of her."

Generally Olivia wasn't thrilled to learn she reminded handsome men of their mothers, however, Luke's compliment pleased her.

But something in his tone made her ask, "Is your mother still living?"

Luke shook his head. "Both my parents passed away a few years ago."

"I'm sorry." Olivia set down her fork, feeling uncomfortable.

"So am I." He nudged the cream pitcher closer to her. "Eat your shortcake."

Olivia sighed and drew it toward her. A minute on the lips, a lifetime on the hips. "I have the distinct impression that you're trying to bribe me into staying."

"You're only mad at me. You don't really want to leave."

Was his ego as big as Texas? "Yes," Olivia said through a mouthful of strawberry shortcake, "I *really* want to leave." She swallowed. "I've had it. Ranching life is not for me."

"Because of the stables?" Luke asked in a quiet voice.

"Yes and no." Olivia hesitated, then decided to elaborate. "You're having a real good time torturing the city slicker. It's obvious you hold me and my profession in complete contempt."

"Not *contempt*," Luke protested, but Olivia figured his heart wasn't in it. He shrugged. "Maybe *one* person..."

She knew he meant John Paul. "Frankly, John Paul isn't easy to work with. He's a demanding, manipulative perfectionist with just enough flashes of brilliance to make him tolerable. However, since you're not in the industry, he probably seems like a complete jackass."

"'Bout sums him up."

Olivia laughed. "Sometimes...egos can become inflated. John Paul whittles them back to size."

"Why do you put up with him?"

Before she answered, Olivia drizzled more cream onto her shortcake. Well, why not? "The ranch depends on you, right? I'll bet you're not winning Mr. Congeniality all the time, either."

"Running a ranch is...different from making a soap opera." There was a slight twist to his mouth as if he didn't consider what John Paul did—and by extension, her—very important.

Olivia dipped a strawberry half into the cream puddle. How decadent. She'd pay later. "I imagine you two have more in common than you realize. A producer is responsible for managing the entire project. Everyone comes to him with problems. Constantly. Big, little, he tackles them all. If he's not strong and decisive, the whole project can fall apart." She popped the strawberry into her mouth and chewed, her expression guileless.

Luke met her gaze, rubbing his upper lip. "You're making me feel ashamed of myself. I couldn't get past that stupid wig of his."

"Shh. That's an outrageously expensive toupee. He'd be appalled if he thought you attributed his lush locks to anything other than fortunate genes."

"Oh, come on," Luke scoffed.

"You should have been there when we all tried to pretend that it was perfectly normal to return from the Christmas holidays with a full head of hair. You see, he'd worn a hat since Thanksgiving. I guess he hoped we'd forget what his head looked like."

Luke threw back his head and laughed.

Olivia found herself laughing, too.

Eventually Luke's laughter quieted to occasional chuckles. "I'll make sure I give him a cowboy hat when he's here to film. Let the toupee rest."

"Oh, a gift from the natives. He'll like that."

As they shared a smile, the evening quiet closed around them. Olivia had eaten every last cream-soaked, calorie-laden crumb.

Now what?

It seemed they'd reached an understanding. They'd part friends. Maybe they'd even get together on one of his New York trips. The possibility made her heart thud.

Luke cleared his throat and stood. "Back to the stables—"

"No." Olivia closed her eyes. "Let's not discuss the stables. This has been the most enjoyable time I've spent here." She opened her eyes to look directly into his. "Please don't spoil it."

Luke said nothing, but held out his hand. Olivia took it and stood, her robe whispering as she stepped away from the chair.

He didn't release her. Instead, he held her hand and regarded her enigmatically.

He was a very attractive man and she was very attracted. There was something about him that was different from any man she'd ever met. Something at once sophisticated and untamed, as though his civility was just a thin veneer.

Something vastly appealing.

His chest rose and fell. Her lips parted. Olivia felt as if she was on the edge of a precipice.

One little tug, and she'd fall into his arms.

Luke didn't tug. But he did lead her into his office.

He was being discreet. They'd have some privacy in there. Wouldn't want to set a bad example for any kids wandering by.

When he crossed the threshold, he flipped on the light, to Olivia's frustration. She was ready to be kissed. She was ready *to* kiss.

So it was exasperating when Luke approached book-filled shelves, scanned the titles, then pulled one down. "This is one of my old ranch-management textbooks from college."

How romantic. *At least give him credit for not pouncing on you, Olivia.* "You can get a degree in ranch management?" Weren't people just born into it?

"Yes."

From where she stood, Olivia saw he held a book on horses. Oh, no. Realistically, with Angel due back as soon as she fed the beasts, there wasn't much time for a full-fledged romantic encounter.

But Luke could certainly engineer a tender moment or two.

He flipped through the pages, then gestured her to the leather couch.

Olivia positioned herself to advantage, resting her arm across the couch back. Her robe fell open, revealing the matching gown beneath. Satin was such a *sensuous* fabric, especially when dyed a lush, flesh-toned pink the way this peignoir was.

Luke sat next to her and placed the book on her knees. "This section is on stable maintenance. And this—" he pinched a wad of pages together "—discusses all the diseases horses contract if you don't maintain your stables."

Olivia blinked into his handsome face, gazing so earnestly at her as he drew her attention to the graphic photographs of ailing horses.

She reviewed the situation: she, Olivia Faraday, leading daytime actress, was arrayed in a satin peignoir and alone with a man who had on previous memorable occasions indicated that he found her attractive. They were inches apart on a cushy leather sofa. And the topic of discussion was not how exciting he found her, but the hooves of horses who had been standing in improperly mucked out stalls.

With illustrations.

"Now do you understand why I was so strict with you?" Luke concluded his lecture.

Olivia closed the book and rose to her feet. "I always understood. However, I didn't think it was appropriate."

She would now stride elegantly to the door, turn and pause in a swirl of satin to deliver her final line in perfect pear-shaped tones. Which she did. "Please tell the cab company that any time after eight o'clock will be fine."

"You're still leaving?" He gestured to the book. "After all this?"

"*Especially* after that."

"You never intended to go through with the whole program, did you?" His voice was cold. Anger stiffened his body as he reshelved the book.

Olivia discovered that she still valued Luke's good opinion. What a silly, weak female she was, buying into the romantic cowboy myth.

"Yes, I did."

He threw her a look of disbelief.

"You're doing something good and great and wonderful and I wanted to do something good and great and wonderful, too. There aren't many genuinely good people in the world. I thought I'd found one. And I continue to believe it."

He stared away from her, his jaw tense. "Will you tell Angel, or shall I?"

"I will."

"I'll arrange for your transportation." He nodded, then turned his back to her and shuffled papers on his desk.

She'd been dismissed. Men always used that power ploy to save face. Well, she'd let him save his handsome face. Olivia smiled to herself. "Good night."

"NO!" ANGEL FLUNG HERSELF in a heap onto the bed.

Olivia had seen this act before. If Angel wanted it to be effective, she'd have to vary the routine.

"If you don't pack tonight, you'll have to pack tomorrow morning. The cab could be here any time after eight."

"I won't leave!"

Olivia examined her oatmeal-colored pantsuit and banged-up pumps. Dirt smudged the hems of the pants, and the gravel had scarred the leather heels. She would be a frayed Diana on the plane. "I'm leaving tomorrow morning. If you want company on the flight back, you're welcome to come with me."

"I'm *not* going! You can't make me!"

Olivia rolled her eyes. Had she ever been this obnoxious as a teenager? "I'm not going to try to make you leave, but Luke can and will."

"I *hate* you!"

Olivia walked into the bathroom, laughing as she went. "Cut the theatrics. You're talking to a pro."

"I hate you, I hate you!" Angel pounded her fist on the mattress with each "hate" she uttered.

Olivia returned with her stinking stable clothes. There was no way she was going to pack them into her suitcase, and they wouldn't dry if she rinsed them out now. Shrugging, she stuffed them into the wastebasket.

"Angel, never lose sight of your goal."

Angel paused, her fist raised in the air. "What are you talking about?"

"What is your goal?"

"Huh?" Down came the fist.

"You're throwing a tantrum on my bed. Why?"

"'Cause I don't want to leave."

"No, no." Olivia shook her head and waved away Angel's explanation. "That's not your goal."

"It isn't?"

"No." Olivia closed the suitcase and dragged it off the bed. "Why did you come here in the first place?"

"Because I want Mr. Luke to give me a college scholarship like my cousin got."

"You're getting warmer. Your goal is to go to college, isn't it?"

Angel nodded as Olivia sat on the bed and tucked her legs beneath her. "And you found a very creative way to achieve your goal. Creative determination. I like that."

"Enough to give me a scholarship?" Angel asked slyly.

"You're learning to play the angles," Olivia noted with approval. "But I'm not sure I want to give you a scholarship."

"Why not? You're a big-deal actress. You make a lot of money." Her lower lip slid forward in a pout.

"I spend a lot of money to stay a 'big-deal actress,'" Olivia said without apology. "I have an agent and a publicist who handles fan mail and requests for pictures—which I pay for. And there are other expenses you wouldn't be interested in. But even though I could probably be your fairy godmother and plop college money in your lap, I won't."

Still pouting, Angel crossed her arms and looked away.

"People don't value things that come too easily. I imagine that's why Luke requires kids to finish his program before he considers them for a scholarship."

"Then why won't you help me?"

"I didn't say I wouldn't help you." Olivia pushed her hair behind her ears. "Actually, that's what I was trying to do. And in the process, I lost sight of *my* goal," she confessed.

She'd recaptured Angel's attention. "What's your goal?"

"To hang on to my job," Olivia said automatically, then sighed. "No." She looked down at her nails, desperately in need of a manicure, and thought of her flighty parents and her aging grandparents, whom she also supported. "My family depends on me. I want to make enough money so they won't have to worry. So *I* won't have to worry."

"Can the weasel-man fire you?"

Olivia chuckled. "He could, but he probably won't. It's his fault I'm here." Olivia noticed Angel's confused face and decided not to go into details about the ethics of publicity hype. "He's mad, though, and I'm sure I'll have to pay for my little rebellion."

Angel looked so distraught that Olivia hastened to reassure her.

"It'll be okay. John Paul and I regularly have our tiffs." She stretched her arms above her head and walked over to the dresser. "Did I tell you my parents are actors, too?"

"No."

"Well, they are and not very good ones." Olivia picked up a bottle of moisturizer and patted on more around her eyes. In the mirror, she didn't see her own reflection, but her mother's reddened eyes.

Her mother had once had a bit part in a second-rate comedy. The scene called for Olivia's mother to be hit in the face with a pie.

The scene was shot over and over again as the star, deliberately, Olivia suspected, fluffed her lines. Olivia, studying on the set with the tutor, recalled listening to the laughter as her mother was hit by pie after pie, carefully cleaning up and redoing her makeup each time.

She could've quit, but she endured the humiliation because they needed money. At the time, Olivia's father wasn't working and the theater where her grandmother was a costumer had shut down. Her grandfather was trying to organize his own Shakespearean troupe.

"I watched my parents put up with some degrading stuff to get work," she explained to Angel. "But I'm not going to." In spite of Luke's explanation about the stables, Olivia knew he'd enjoyed her struggles the past few days.

Enjoyed them too much.

"So." She turned to face the silent girl on her bed. "I'm going home tomorrow. You can come with me or not. Either way, I'll still help you."

The next morning, Olivia sat in the den nursing a second cup of coffee and reading a day-old newspaper.

It was nine o'clock. Had Luke forgotten to arrange their transportation?

Olivia decided she'd allow another half an hour and if she didn't see either Luke or a cab by then, she'd call for one herself.

She glanced at Angel's closed door. There hadn't been a peep out of her. Olivia had no idea if the girl planned to go with her this morning.

Luke hadn't made an appearance, either. Obviously Olivia was the Bluebonnet pariah.

Wasn't he even going to say goodbye?

Much as she didn't want to admit it, she'd be hurt if he ignored her departure. He was honest and decent, handsome, available and, she'd thought, interested.

She tossed the newspaper down. *Are you nuts? What kind of relationship would you have, anyway?* Maybe Luke saw what she saw. Olivia was no rancher. She'd be useless out here.

Her place was in New York.

And even if she wanted to throw away everything she'd worked for, she would still have her family responsibilities.

So Luke could come to New York, right?

Wrong. Olivia stood and wandered over to the front window. Looking out on the rolling Texas hills, she knew Luke would never be happy in New York. He'd never willingly give up Bluebonnet Ranch.

And beautiful and peaceful as the ranch was, Olivia recognized that she needed the stimulation of New York. Of her work.

Such was life.

Time to get on with it. Olivia was about to search for Luke herself, when she picked out a dust cloud on the horizon. A taxi?

After a few minutes, she realized it was a long black car.

A limousine.

"Angel! Come look at this."

The door opened and a silent Angel joined her at the window.

"Do you see that? Have you ever ridden in a limo before?"

Angel shook her head.

"Well? Are you coming with me or not?"

"I'm coming." But she didn't sound happy.

So Luke had decided to send Olivia off in style. Or was he merely pointing out their differences?

Whatever, she wasn't one to refuse limo rides.

"I'll get my suitcase," Angel said dully.

"Oh, no." Olivia stopped her as the car pulled up directly in front of the ranch house. A chauffeur emerged. "See? The driver will carry your bag."

But the driver walked around to the passenger side of the car and opened it.

For Mr. Collingsworth.

CHAPTER EIGHT

AND MR. COLLINGSWORTH was followed by a Chanel-suited woman who could only be Mrs. Collingsworth. Olivia recognized her from the photographs in Luke's office.

Apparently no one else had noticed the Collingsworths' arrival. Olivia pressed her face to the window and tried to see the bunkhouse. All was quiet.

"He's coming to get me!" Angel cried.

"Hush. You were leaving, anyway."

Angel sniffed, but calmed down. "He doesn't look mad."

Olivia watched the man's progress as he climbed the stairs. No, he didn't look angry. Yet.

How should she play this? Olivia wondered as she answered the door.

"It's Diana D'Angelo!" The slim, gray-haired woman at Mr. Collingsworth's side gasped and clutched her husband's arm.

Olivia had her answer. Mrs. Collingsworth expected Diana. Except Olivia felt she'd never looked less like Diana D'Angelo. Not even when Diana had been kidnapped and imprisoned in a cave for two horrible weeks had her makeup been less than perfect.

In fact, right now, Olivia didn't even look like Olivia.

"You must be Mrs. Collingsworth," she said in her Diana-playing-lady-of-the-manor voice.

"Oh, I'm so thrilled!" gushed Mrs. Collingsworth. Once inside the house, she grasped Olivia's hand and seemed disinclined to let it go. "I've been watching *Lovers and Liars* ever since your second marriage."

"The real second marriage or the sham wedding arranged by the fake Italian count?"

"Wasn't that a real marriage?" Mrs. Collingsworth looked stricken.

"Oh, no. Remember, he only wanted a way to smuggle pearls out of Italy?"

Mrs. Collingsworth thought for a moment, then nodded vigorously. "Yes! He'd had them sewn into your veil and then told everyone it had belonged to his grandmother." She finally dropped Olivia's hand and turned to her husband. "The wedding was on his yacht, you see, and no one suspected anything until they were in international waters."

Mr. Collingsworth smiled indulgently.

It had been a wonderful story line, Olivia remembered, and one that had occurred at least eight years ago. The cast had spent a week in Venice. The ratings had soared, and Diana D'Angelo had become firmly entrenched as a major character.

From would-be countess to a ranch hand. Where had she gone wrong?

"And this must be our little stowaway!" boomed Mr. Collingsworth. He sounded as jovial as a department store Santa Claus—and just as fake. Olivia didn't remember him being jovial at all.

"This is Angel," she said. Poor Angel looked as if she'd bolt at the first opportunity.

"Angel, eh? Well, you haven't acted like an angel, have you?"

Angel began to shake, even more when the screen door opened and Luke stalked inside.

His mouth was set in a grim line; his eyes flashed with scorn. Then he noticed the Collingsworths. Recovering quickly, he was smiling and holding out his hand in greeting by the time they turned toward him.

Olivia had been deliberately studying his face and could guess that Luke had spotted the limousine and thought she'd ordered it. He was all bent out of shape and was coming to tell her so. The Collingsworths' visit was obviously unexpected.

"I was just talking to our little cowgirl here." Mr. Collingsworth lowered his head and spoke sternly to Angel. "Young lady, your family has been worried about you."

Most likely they'd appeared on his doorstep screaming lawsuit.

"I left a note," Angel mumbled, hanging her head.

"Surprised I didn't hear about this from you, Luke." Such a deceptively mild tone. His tone and the way Mr. Collingsworth stared at Angel while he addressed Luke alerted Olivia that Mr. Collingsworth didn't like surprises.

However, Luke didn't allow Mr. Collingsworth to put him on the defensive. He said nothing until his silence caused the older man to look at him. And then he only responded with an equally mild, "Everything's under control."

"I very much hope so. A scandal wouldn't do the foundation any good at all."

Angel was crying. She made no sound, but tears rolled down her cheeks and dripped off her chin. Luke couldn't see her or he would have responded, Olivia knew.

"Scandal? Is having a girl here *that* unusual?" she asked, careful to inject surprised innocence into her voice. "I wasn't aware that the Bluebonnet program was for boys only."

"Of course it's for boys," Mr. Collingsworth stated.

"Really?" Olivia arched an eyebrow. "Everything I've read about your organization has referred to 'youth.' I didn't realize you excluded girls. That's discrimination, isn't it?"

As she spoke, Olivia moved across the room to Angel. "It's a long drive from Austin, and I'll bet the Collingsworths would like a glass of lemonade." She put her arm around Angel's shoulders and urged her toward the kitchen. "I don't know what it is, but the lemonade here is the best I've ever tasted," she chattered. Just before she nudged Angel through the doorway, Olivia bent and whispered, "Don't worry."

She came back to an animated Mrs. Collingsworth. "I've told you over and over again," she chided her husband. "But you won't listen to me."

"A ranch is no place for girls." Mr. Collingsworth's face was turning a mottled red. "*You* tell her," he appealed to Luke.

Luke shrugged and perched easily on the arm of an overstuffed chair, gesturing for the rest of them to sit down. Far from appearing concerned, he looked as though he were prepared to be entertained. "I had a group of girls here once."

"*Once?* That's not what it says in the pamphlet I read. Did you know that?" Olivia asked him as she sat in a rustic twig chair next to the Collingsworths. It was as uncomfortable as it looked.

"I have no objection to girls," Luke said carefully. "But I generally take what I get. And I've been getting boys."

"I see." Olivia crossed her arms and gazed at Mr. Collingsworth.

"Boys *need* this sort of experience," Mr. Collingsworth insisted.

"You both are going to get into trouble with some government agency or another unless you allow more girls to participate in the Bluebonnet program," Mrs. Collingsworth pronounced. "Besides, it would do girls a world of good."

"I can't find any girls to come!" Mr. Collingsworth bellowed.

"Nonsense. There's one in the kitchen making lemonade right now." To Olivia's amazement, Mrs. Collingsworth continued to challenge her husband. "Furthermore, you and Luke owe Diana D'Angelo a huge debt of gratitude for chaperoning her or you would've been embroiled in scandal up to the hair in your ears!"

Olivia immediately stared at Mr. Collingsworth's ears, which were red on the tops. She was rather disappointed not to see tufts of hair.

Mrs. Collingsworth turned to Olivia. "We've had so very many reporters asking about the Bluebonnet program. And all due to your participation."

"I imagine the *Lovers and Liars* publicity department had something to do with that." Olivia was unsure if she was sharing credit or blame.

"A *lot* to do with it," Luke commented.

"Can you imagine how awkward it would have been if you had that one little girl here with only men around?"

"I didn't know she was a girl!" protested Mr. Collingsworth.

"She couldn't have stayed here by herself," Luke said. "I would've sent her back."

"And how would *that* have looked to the press?" Mrs. Collingsworth asked in ringing tones. She grasped Olivia's hand once more. "When you saw what was needed, you offered your precious time without hesitation." She squeezed Olivia's hand. "I always knew that deep down inside, Diana was a good girl."

Diana again. Olivia hesitated, involuntarily looking at Luke. He was amused at her predicament. So amused he could barely keep from laughing.

This wasn't funny. How could Olivia break the news that she, Diana and Angel were leaving? It was obvious that Luke wasn't going to help her.

"Mrs. Collingsworth, you're exaggerating my contribution to the program. In fact, I—"

"And that goodness," Mrs. Collingsworth continued, undeterred, "persuaded me to give Diana another chance, in *spite* of my husband's opposition." Mrs. Collingsworth beamed at them all.

Mr. Collingsworth cleared his throat. "I don't like to be proved wrong, but I have to agree with my wife. She kept saying Diana could change, and now I see she's right." Both Collingsworths radiated approval.

Perhaps she should reconsider leaving, Olivia thought. Faced with the admiring gazes of the Collingsworths, she felt trapped. Once more, her eyes sought Luke's.

His were filled with a devilish glee. He knew she was being backed into a corner and was enjoying every minute of it.

The sound of tires crunching on gravel broke the silence. A horn beeped twice.

Luke squinted out the window. "Your taxi's here, Diana."

Olivia shot him a venomous glance, to which he responded with an innocent expression.

"Taxi?" Mrs. Collingsworth dropped Olivia's hand. "You're leaving?"

"Yes, she is," Luke responded. Cheerfully.

Dismay spread across the Collingsworths' faces. "But what about the girl?" asked Mr. Collingsworth.

"Angel? Oh, she's leaving, too." Luke, normally laconic, had turned into a veritable font of information. Olivia glared at him.

"Diana?" Mrs. Collingsworth blinked, her gaze sweeping over Olivia's pantsuit and scuffed pumps. Inappropriate ranch clothes. "What is the meaning of this?"

The meaning was that Olivia was going to have to stay or Diana would never recover from her coma, that much was clear. And she didn't need a script to figure it out or know that Luke would make her grovel.

She'd be on permanent stable duty.

She'd have to eat fried food.

She'd have to ride a horse for hours at a time.

She'd never walk straight again.

And the absolute *worst* part of it was she'd have to beg for the privilege of being tortured.

"Diana?" Mrs. Collingsworth choked, as if she were about to burst into tears.

"I *am* sorry we can't visit longer, but Angel and I are going...shopping." Olivia didn't look at Luke. She couldn't look at Luke, but every nerve she possessed screamed at him to play along with her.

"Shopping?" The Collingsworths and Luke all spoke at once. Olivia hoped Luke's voice was drowned out.

She laughed an artificial little Diana laugh and picked up her purse. "You remember that I only planned to be here for a few days. I need more clothes. Angel could use some more jeans, too." Olivia stood and smiled through gritted teeth, then faced Luke. Well? Would he support her? And if so, what was it going to cost her?

He swung his booted foot back and forth, drawing out the suspense. One look at his expression and Olivia knew she'd pay a high price for changing her mind. He *did* know she'd changed her mind, didn't he?

He opened his mouth. Olivia held her breath.

And Mrs. Collingsworth gushed. "Oh, I'm so relieved!" She sagged against her husband and clenched a fist against her heart. "I thought...I thought you were leaving the ranch. For *good*."

"I can see how you might have had that impression," Olivia said dryly.

"And that would have been just awful." Mrs. Collingsworth gave a mournful shake of her head.

The taxi's horn sounded again. Luke slid off the chair arm and sauntered to the screen door. "Hang loose for a minute," he called before returning to his perch.

"For me to have misjudged Diana so would have meant we'd have to rethink her continuing role on *Lovers and Liars*," Mrs. Collingsworth continued.

All right already, Olivia thought. Message received, loud and clear.

"And...and—" Mrs. Collingsworth gazed at her husband "—I just couldn't bear to sponsor *Lovers and Liars* without Diana."

Hello, what's this? "Are you saying that without me, you'll withdraw your sponsorship of our show?" Olivia asked.

"Why, Diana's the only reason we sponsored it."

Olivia smiled. Beamed. "If Diana isn't on the show, she can't inherit a ranch, can she? So there would be no reason for *Lovers and Liars* to film on location or to pay Luke for the rights." It was important to emphasize that fact, in case Luke missed it. "And really no reason to run the public-service announcements about the foundation, either."

"Oh, dear." This had obviously not occurred to Mrs. Collingsworth.

Olivia looked across the room to a wary Luke. His leg no longer swung. "It's been my experience that network contracts have contingency clauses," she said. "You haven't spent your contract-signing money already, have you, Luke?"

He hesitated noticeably before answering. "There were some equipment repairs that couldn't wait," he admitted finally.

Oh, she wished she had a camera to record his expression the precise instant the balance of power shifted. She would savor his look for the rest of her days.

"You can't just walk off the show. What about *your* contract?" Luke asked.

"Up for renewal. My agent's still negotiating it," she answered sweetly.

"You'd better be nice to her, then, Luke." Mr. Collingsworth chuckled. Olivia felt like dancing behind the corpulent Mr. Collingsworth and sticking out her tongue at Luke.

Ha-ha, she'd sing. *No more fried food, no more smelly stables, no more—*

"If Diana's out of a job, you're out of a job, right?" Luke asked her directly.

How fortunate she hadn't given into her childish impulse to gloat. How unfortunate that Luke understood this very important point. The balance of power was equal.

"Here's the lemonade," said a soft voice behind her.

Angel. She'd forgotten all about Angel.

"Our taxi's here." Olivia took the tray from Angel and set it on the coffee table, then grabbed Angel's arm and hustled her toward the doorway.

"But my things!" she protested.

"That's right, we're going to buy lots of new things," Olivia said loudly. "Get in the cab, and I'll explain later," she murmured to an astonished Angel.

Luke held the door open for her. Happily, the girl was bright and did as she was told at once. With a minuscule jerk of his head, Luke signaled Olivia for a conference.

It would have to be a short one. She said a hurried goodbye to the Collingsworths and met him at the bottom of the stairs.

"You're staying?" he demanded, without preliminaries.

"I don't have a choice."

"Sure you do."

"Yeah, right."

They wasted precious seconds simply staring at each other. Olivia watched the rise and fall of his chest. He was dragging in air as if he'd just run a race, and he looked into her eyes as if he could read her thoughts.

"I need the cash they'll pay for the rights to film at Bluebonnet," he said bluntly. "And I need it now."

"I need my job," she returned, equally blunt. "I've got my own cash-flow problems."

Olivia couldn't remember the last time she'd had a lay-your-cards-on-the-table discussion. Usually negotiations in her industry were obscured by threats, subtle hype and highly subjective judgments of worth.

"If we work together, then we'll both get what we want." Luke stated the obvious.

"Agreed." Olivia inclined her head. "*If* you understand that I won't tolerate being humiliated anymore."

"Now hold on—"

Olivia slashed her hand in the air. They were wasting time. "You thought it was real funny to assign the *glamorous actress* all the worst chores."

"Somebody had to do them."

"And you made sure that somebody was me." Olivia pointed to herself. "I knew what you were doing, but I played along to show you that you'd misjudged me."

She was aware of the passing minutes and that the Collingsworths would surely investigate momentarily. Still, this had to be said. "I read the newspaper articles you've got framed in your office—the ones where you're quoted as saying the world has stereotyped the kids you bring here? That's what you did to me. You say they should be treated with respect. I deserve the same."

There. She'd said her piece.

His eyes narrowed. "You want to be treated exactly the same as they are?"

"No, I don't. We're here for different reasons."

"Oh, I get it." He crossed his arms over his chest. "You want to hole up all day in the ranch house and put goop on your face and paint your toenails. You'll demand your own chef, but you won't eat anything other than a lettuce leaf and foreign water."

He didn't get it at all. Maybe he didn't want to get it.

"Are you confusing me with Diana D'Angelo?" she asked sweetly. "Many people do."

"I know exactly who you are."

"A stereotypical New York actress?"

Luke started to respond, then stopped, an arrested expression on his face. Exhaust fumes clouded around them accompanied by the hum of the cab engine. The morning sun cut through the cool air. Olivia stood her ground. She would not give on this point. Not even to keep her job. She tilted her chin and made sure Luke could see the resolve on her face.

"Ouch," he said finally, uncrossing his arms and shoving his hands into his back pockets.

Olivia relaxed.

"You caught me," he said, and smiled. Really smiled.

And Olivia forgave him instantly. Completely. Her anger evaporated. Poof. Gone.

That smile should be registered as a lethal weapon.

She was used to men who smiled. They smiled perfect, practiced smiles on command. Smiles that showed even white teeth, yet didn't accentuate the wrinkles around their eyes. Smiles that appeared at the first sign of a photographer. Smiles designed to seduce the camera—and women.

Luke's smile was lopsided. One side of his mouth raced upward and the other never quite stretched as far. His eyes crinkled, the skin easily creasing along familiar lines.

It was a heartbreaker of a smile. One of those smiles that enticed you do things you later regretted.

"We'll talk details after you get back," he said, opening the cab door.

"We're coming *back?* We're going on the camping trip?" Angel looked as though she'd been granted her heart's desire. And Olivia supposed she had been. She nodded and Angel sagged against the torn vinyl seat, her eyes closed.

Obviously she hadn't had any confidence in Olivia's promises of help.

"Take them to Llano," Luke instructed the driver, then explained to Olivia, "If you go all the way to Austin, you'll spend more on cab fare than clothes." He shut the door and leaned down to the window. "Make sure you buy a good pair of boots." He glanced at Angel. "For her, too."

"Will I know a good pair of boots when I see them?"

Luke squatted down until his face was level with hers. "Go to Willie's Western Wear. I'll call ahead and tell them you're coming."

"Lady, are we going anywhere or not? The meter's running."

"So you'll get paid. What's the problem?" she snapped. Cabbies were the same everywhere.

"Olivia?"

"Hmm?" It was the first time he'd said her name. It rolled like a wave across his tongue. He had a drawl, but not an extreme west Texas twang like Tom from the set crew. Just enough to take the edge off the consonants.

"You *are* coming back, aren't you?"

So he wasn't completely sure of her. Good. She opened her mouth, intending to make a flippant remark, but was caught by the intensity of his gaze.

He needed the production money. *Really* needed it.

Olivia remembered the conversation with the Collingsworths and realized that they didn't know how bad Luke's financial difficulties were. She also knew he was a proud man and wouldn't willingly admit any of this.

Pride was something Olivia understood and admired.

She lowered her voice, added an Austrian accent and said, "I'll be back."

CHAPTER NINE

OLIVIA FARADAY had been suckered by a smile.

True, it was one heck of a smile, but after jouncing on Star for the past two days, Olivia found that the luster of Luke's smile had dimmed.

Was preserving her role as Diana worth this torment? Was *anything* worth taking potty breaks behind bushes?

Star, as was her wont, veered from the path to eat grass. "Star," groaned Olivia. No amount of yanking, kicking, pleading or threatening could budge the horse.

Olivia was quite willing to try bribery, but she was out of sugar cubes, and feeding Star sugar would've meant dismounting. The last time Olivia dismounted, her legs rebelled, and she didn't think she'd ever get on the horse again.

As it was, she ambled along at the end of the line of horses, pretending that's where she preferred to ride, anyway. Luke rode at the head of the line, of course. Their fearless leader. At one with the land.

Olivia had inhaled grit for two days. She hadn't bathed in two days. She was about as one with the land as she could get.

She failed to see the allure.

She was blistered and burned, dirty and dejected. There were no bubbles on the trail. She was not a happy camper.

Luke, however, was in his element. Even worse, he was a morning person, eager to convey the delights of the new day to everyone.

What was wrong with her that she couldn't share his enthusiasm?

Oh, the scenery was beautiful. Wildflowers bloomed everywhere. The camera crew would go nuts. Bluebonnets flourished in clumps and fields, along with bright orange-red Indian paintbrush and the occasional buttercup.

And cactus. Mean little scrubby cactus that hid behind innocent bushes and stabbed unwary victims, or scratched the legs of those riders whose horses were on unauthorized search-and-eat missions.

"Prickly pear," Luke had said when he'd ridden to investigate her yelp yesterday. "That's why I told you to wear the boots."

No sympathy whatsoever. She hadn't been wearing the boots because they pinched. And they pinched because they weren't broken in. At that rate, the boots were going to break in her feet.

Deeply frustrated, Olivia yanked Star's reins. The horse, still munching weeds, raised her head.

"Star, you can't eat that stuff. You'll get sick." She eyed the plants dangling out of the horse's mouth. "I think." Unless they had flowers attached, all weeds looked alike to Olivia. "I can't remember what the bad stuff is anymore. But you've lived here your whole life, so you ought to remember, right?"

Olivia pulled the reins to the left, trying to urge her placid horse back onto the path.

Star turned her head, but didn't move. Eight youthful horsemen, led by the lone rancher, clip-clopped onward, leaving her behind. "Give me a limo any day," she muttered.

The sky was a clear blue from which the sun shone down. Brightly. Hotly. Intensely. All those harmful, aging rays were soaking into her skin. Olivia settled her hat more firmly on her head.

That was another thing. No matter what Luke said, she did like the hat. It was a beautiful teal green with peacock feathers decorating the crown and brim. Vivid jewel tones complemented her dark coloring, so why shouldn't she wear the hat? It was a flattering hat and made her feel pretty. And right now, Olivia desperately needed to feel pretty.

But Luke had hooted when he saw it. "That's a show hat for city slickers. Willie's been trying to unload that thing for three years."

Stung, Olivia had retorted, "It'll keep the sun off my head. That's what it's for, isn't it?" How dared he criticize her beautiful hat? Was there some ranch fashion guide that said only earth tones were allowed?

Resting her arms, aching from her tug-of-war with Star, she checked the other riders' progress and saw them clustered around a large bush. Oh, no, had they finally found a cow? Ostensibly, they were hunting for cattle that had wandered away from the herd during roundup. To Olivia's great relief, they hadn't found any. She was only beginning to tolerate horses.

"Star," she begged her recalcitrant horse. "Please catch up with them. It's so humiliating when Luke has to ride back and get me."

Sure enough, rhythmic clopping announced that Luke and Vulcan were on their way.

"Star!" Olivia spat out in complete disgust. "Don't you have any pride?" She kicked the horse's ribs. Of course kicking did no good whatsoever because Star was so fat Olivia's legs were already stretched out too far to get any momentum built up.

Star chewed contentedly. Olivia threw back her shoulders as if enjoying the view. She began to hum a little tune, then stopped abruptly. No need to overdo it.

The cavalry arrived. "Howdy." Luke tipped his hat to her, eyes twinkling.

"Good morning," Olivia said civilly in return. "Lovely day, isn't it? I was just sitting here breathing in all this clean, fresh air." She inhaled deeply.

"You've been breathing a lot lately." He eyed her chest. "You breathe very well."

Olivia exhaled, blowing the air out through her mouth. "Years of practice."

Luke hooked a thumb over his shoulder. "We found a jack-rabbit nest."

"How nice. And I found these lovely..." Olivia gestured toward the clump Star had been investigating.

"Weeds?" He grinned and leaned forward to grasp Star's bridle. "You shouldn't let her get away with this," he said as he led Olivia and Star back to the group.

"I don't appear to have any choice."

"You need to show her who's boss."

"She *knows* who's boss," Olivia grumbled.

Luke laughed.

"So glad you're amused."

He threw a glance back at her. "You *are* pretty funny."

Olivia didn't reply. She didn't even have the satisfaction of knowing he'd flounder in her world—her New York world. No, he actually hobnobbed with the social elite. *She'd* never been asked to the Bluebonnet Ball, which was attended by the crustiest of the upper crust.

"Hey." He slowed, then stopped out of earshot of Angel and the boys. Star took the opportunity to graze again. "Has the place grown on you any?"

"I wouldn't be surprised if *something* was growing on me," Olivia muttered.

Luke leaned over his saddle horn and gazed around him. "No matter how many times I wake up to these hills, I never get tired of seeing them and knowing they're mine."

Olivia ignored the hills and admired his profile. He was one good-looking man. She wouldn't mind waking up and knowing he was hers.

"There isn't much I wouldn't do to keep them."

"Like put up with me?" He was reminding her that the ranch would always come first with him. He didn't have to rub it in.

"You're not so bad," he said, squinting off into the distance.

"Gee, thanks."

He shook his head slightly before turning back to her. "The money from your show is going to save my hide. We've had two miserable winters in a row with a drought in between. The cattle couldn't graze and feed costs soared. Repairs ate up the rest of my cash." A corner of his mouth lifted. "That's the thing about this business. One year you're rich, the next you're standing in line at the bank. Of course, if you're standing in line, so's every other rancher in these parts."

"Couldn't you sell some land?"

Luke shook his head. "Little bits and pieces aren't going to do anybody any good. 'Sides, I ought to be fine by the end of the summer. It's holding out until then that's the problem."

Olivia had known Luke was on thin financial ice, but she hadn't known it was lose-the-ranch thin. She'd bet the Collingsworths didn't know, either. "And how many college educations are you paying for?"

"I dunno." Luke shrugged, then cupped a hand around his mouth. "Time for lunch!"

Ah, the old change-the-subject ploy. She'd allow it this time. Three of the boys had dismounted, anyway. The rest followed suit, eagerly digging in their saddlebags for sandwiches. Angel glanced in their direction, then wandered off to sit on a rock, partially shaded by a scrubby bush.

Olivia shifted on Star. "You're so incredibly *good.* Good people make me nervous."

"*You're* a good person." Luke's gaze held hers as he spoke. "You could've gone back to New York and left me to deal with Angel."

"She caught me in a weak moment," Olivia mumbled, shifting again. Her bottom was numb.

"Well, I'm grateful. We're trying to get public support for the Bluebonnet program, and we don't need a scandal."

"'Scandal' is a little harsh."

He sighed. "You'd be surprised."

Olivia thought of the scandal-sniffing Bettina from *Soap Bubbles*. "I probably wouldn't."

"The Collingsworths are ultraconservative. They don't like notoriety."

"Ha. Then why are they sponsoring a soap opera? We thrive on notoriety."

Luke reached for her reins. "Been any changes since they've become sponsors?"

Changes? Didn't he know? "The entire writing staff was fired. Diana has an uncharacteristic story line. And I'm out here in the wilds of Texas eating too much white bread."

Chuckling, Luke helped her dismount. "They do like to meddle. But in this case I'm glad."

His hands rested lightly on her waist. Olivia licked dry lips. "Because of the money you'll get?"

His gaze held hers as he shook his head. "Because I met you."

Uh-oh. Olivia's heart thumped. No, no, no and no.

Luke slowly let his hands fall away, and Olivia's heart slowed.

This was neither the time nor the place to acknowledge the desire she saw in his eyes. Not to him and not to herself. In fact, she'd wrapped her feelings for him in a box and marked it Do Not Open.

"Thanks," she said inadequately, and held out her hands for the reins.

He silently surrendered them to her, and she looked away as she tied them to the bush.

Olivia was afraid that there never would be a right time or right place to encourage anything deeper to develop between them. The longer she stayed at Bluebonnet, the more she realized that Luke couldn't survive without the ranch.

And she couldn't survive *on* the ranch.

Oh, he was handsome and disgustingly altruistic, in spite of his current cash-flow problems. But he was also living his life exactly the way he wanted to. She'd watched the changes in him as they rode away from the ranch house. Tension eased, the frown line between his eyebrows smoothed. He was happy and content. He was in his element.

He was a true cowboy.

And she was a city girl. Yes, being on the ranch was relaxing—for a change. A temporary change. Not a lifestyle change.

She could fall in love with this man. But he only existed here, on the ranch. Asking Luke to live in New York would change him, destroy the very essence of what attracted her to him.

And what about her? Could she chuck everything and repeat the past two weeks over and over again? Become a... Olivia hesitated to think the words, then mentally drew a deep breath.

Ranch wife?

That's where the relationship would lead. She and Luke were both past the fling stages in their lives. They both knew what they wanted, and they both knew what they wanted in a spouse.

Any woman Luke married would be a ranch wife.

Olivia tested the role.

And shuddered.

Regret nearly overwhelmed her. That involuntary shudder was a warning: heartbreak ahead.

Star turned her head to investigate as Olivia retrieved her unappetizing lunch. "This is *mine*. You've been eating all day."

Patting Star's rump, Luke rejoined Olivia. "You aren't much of an outdoors person, are you?"

Olivia bit into her sandwich, hoping for baked turkey and getting a mouthful of bologna. She washed it down with warm water from her canteen. "No, I'm not." Better to be frank and emphasize their differences. She knew he wanted her to tell him that she was beginning to like being outdoors all day and night. That she enjoyed camping. That she was interested in the ranch critters and their habits. That she enjoyed living in a *National Geographic* special.

But she didn't.

And she could tell he was disappointed.

"But you know what I do like? Walking down Forty-fifth Street at eleven when the shows let out. All the lights and people, their clothes... The excitement when they've seen a really good show or the disappointment when one closes early."

"But it's not real," he protested, confirming her suspicions.

"Sure it is!" Olivia gestured with her sandwich. "I remember the suspense of staying up late with my parents after an opening night. We'd wait at a party for the first reviews in the early editions of the papers. When the reviews were good, it was incredible. We'd all celebrate, and nobody could sleep the rest of the night."

"Somebody's opinion could make you feel like that?"

"Yes."

"You'd prefer artificial lights to the stars?"

She nodded. "They're just as pretty."

Luke stared at her as if she were an unknown species. *Shallow,* she could hear him thinking. Yes, he'd hate New York.

"Hey, chickie-mama. Want some company?" The short, tough-looking boy Olivia thought of as the boys' leader sauntered over to Angel and plopped himself down next to her. She scooted away. He slid after her, reached his arm across her shoulders and hauled her close to him.

"Leave me alone!" She removed the arm and glared at him.

"Hey, babe," called a taller youth with a double-pierced earlobe. "You need a man to protect you?"

Not again. Olivia glanced at Luke. He appeared to be ignoring the scene across the path, but Olivia knew he was aware of what was going on.

"She's got Rafe." The first boy pointed to himself. "And I'm enough man for any chick."

Wearing a disgusted expression, Angel grabbed the remains of her lunch and came over to sit next to Olivia and Luke.

"Don't go 'way, mama," Rafe called.

"Your ugly face scared her off," the other boy, Joel, taunted him.

Rafe jumped to his feet, fists balled.

Luke swore under his breath and stood, brushing off the seat of his jeans.

"You okay, Angel?" Olivia asked.

"Jerks," Angel said succinctly.

Unfortunately this was the third time this scene or a variation had been played.

Rafe and Joel faced each other, chests thrust forward, like a couple of bantam roosters. The other boys silently watched the struggle for power.

Olivia's patience had long since fled. She didn't know how Luke stood it day in and day out. If it were up to her, she'd clunk their heads together.

If it were up to her, she admitted in a rush of honesty, they wouldn't be here at all.

"LET'S PITCH CAMP for the night."

Luke was calling a halt earlier than he had the last two nights, but Olivia wasn't going to complain.

Joel and Rafe had continued sniping at each other the entire afternoon. The other five boys were watchful.

They were ready to support the leader, just as soon as they could figure out who he was.

Angel and Olivia had deliberately ridden farther and farther back from the group. Olivia could tell the boys' posturing was meant to impress Angel. However, Angel was blind to anyone but Luke, and her near hero worship was getting on Olivia's nerves.

Of course, just about everything got on her nerves these days.

She was trying, really trying, but her physical discomforts and the endless squabbling canceled out the land's beauty.

She slid down from Star and led her to the other horses. If the same schedule held, the supply van would arrive by the time they pitched their tents.

"Rafe, tend to the horses." Luke began assigning chores as he did with every stop. "Joel, take two of the others and gather firewood. A front is coming through, and it's going to get chilly later tonight."

Olivia fanned herself with her hat. Chilly sounded just fine.

"Ladies, you can make the fire circle and help cook supper."

Angel started gathering rocks before Luke finished speaking.

"Man, why do they get the easy stuff?" Rafe complained.

"Because you were responsible for the noon meal." Luke let that sink in. Everyone, hungry from the thin sandwiches that had passed for lunch, stared at Rafe. "I'm starving, and I want good food and plenty of it," Luke continued. "I know Angel can cook."

"Excuse me," Olivia said, ignoring the fact that Luke had failed to praise her culinary abilities. "Cooking is just as hard as any of the other chores." There. A blow for feminism.

Luke's eyes swiveled toward her. "So you'd like to trade for a stint at chopping wood?" There was a dangerous you-want-it-tough-I-can-make-it-tough tone to his voice.

She had no doubt that he could. "Not this time." What was the good of suffering for feminism if no one was around to appreciate it?

She was saved from further charges of special treatment by the arrival of the Bluebonnet supply van.

Although the group was on their own for the entire day, a van carrying food and supplies met them at a prearranged site each evening.

On the longer treks, once the kids had adjusted, the supply visits were further apart. The whole point of the camping trip was to teach everyone self-reliance, as well as responsibility to a group. If one person let the group down, everyone suffered. The plan was that the kids would transfer these feelings of responsibility from the group to society as a whole.

Olivia tugged her pup tent from Star's back, carefully checking the outer perimeter of the campsite for wild cows.

Thank goodness this wasn't a two-week trip. Groups on the longer wilderness trips later in the summer would inspect the outer fenced boundaries running next to the highway and make needed repairs. It was real, honest-to-goodness work.

But it wasn't Olivia's work.

She already had a job. A job with which she supported her grandparents and heavily subsidized her parents.

A job she loved as much as Luke loved his ranch.

BUT A JOB OLIVIA would abandon in a minute if all her ranch time could be spent like this—with Luke, outside at night, sitting next to a flickering fire under a velvet sky embroidered with stars.

"The stars at night really are big and bright, deep in the heart of Texas," she said, fighting the urge to lean against him.

Once the sun set, the air rapidly cooled. The squabbling among the boys had ceased as each camper retreated to his own tent to sleep. Luke and Olivia kept watch, more because they wanted to than because of potential danger.

Except for the spitting fire and the soft nickering of the horses, the night was quiet.

Luke poked the fire sending sparks shooting skyward. He watched their progress as they blinked out. "Now, how can you tell me your city lights are prettier than those stars?"

Olivia hugged her knees to her chest and tilted her head back. "Not prettier. Different."

"I'll say."

"This is peaceful. Serene. Reassuringly familiar."

"I hear boring in there."

Well, that was true. But each night, boredom took longer and longer to set in.

Luke squatted next to the fire and tossed pieces of gnarled brushwood on it.

The sight of him, silhouetted against the rising flames, surrounded by the curtain of darkness, evoked elemental feelings. Primitive emotions.

And very basic desires.

She, who had negotiated nearly half her life on her own, relying solely on herself, felt cherished and safe by Luke's simple act of tending to the fire. She enjoyed surrendering some of her independence. Something about communing with the land called to long-forgotten survival instincts—the weaker female seeking the protection of the stronger male.

With the fire resuscitated, Luke lowered himself next to her. The fire popped, and Olivia jumped, drawing his attention. They gazed at each other, Luke's eyes almost navy blue in the firelight. Shadows danced across his face in wild abandon. Olivia shivered. Without a word, Luke dropped his arm around her shoulders and sheltered her next to his heart.

They sat that way without talking, Olivia listening contentedly to the steady rhythm of his pulse. New York, with its lights, movement, excitement and pressure, was another world.

In her mind, Olivia approached the box marked Do Not Open, the one where she'd hidden her feelings for Luke.

"Look!" he said suddenly, and pointed.

Far away one of the lights fell from the sky.

"Quick, make a wish," he urged.

Watching his face as he followed the trail of the shooting star, Olivia made her wish.

Then she unwrapped the box in her mind.

"Did you make a wish?" he asked, smiling down at her.

"Yes," she answered, holding his gaze.

His smile faded, but the light from the stars was reflected in his eyes. "Did we wish for the same thing?"

Olivia tilted her head against his shoulder, her mouth inches from his. "Let's find out."

His lips met hers in slow motion, a kiss of discovery, not possession.

Mesquite smoke scented his hair, barbecue spiced his mouth. Her fingers caressed his beard-roughened jaw; his caressed her wind-burned cheek. It was a kiss of unfolding tenderness, a contrast to the rugged land.

It wasn't their first kiss, but it was the kiss Olivia wanted to remember. Always. Forever. This kiss was as different from the other as . . . night and day.

The day kiss had been long on technique and short on emotion, although Olivia certainly couldn't fault his technique. But it had been a kiss for the cameras, a kiss to impress the star.

And Olivia had been too aware of the photographers, the reporters and the passionate jolt to her senses to explore her feelings then.

With this kiss, Luke demanded that she acknowledge her feelings, as well as his.

And the feelings nearly overwhelmed her—unfamiliar yearnings, basic, instinctive, timeless. A desire to give up everything and fuse her soul with his.

Heat seeped through her as she responded to his touch on a primitive level that shocked her. She was woman, he was man, and nothing else mattered.

A moan signaled her surrender.

At the sound, Luke buried his hand underneath her hair, holding her close as he deepened the kiss.

This was a possessive kiss.

Olivia reveled in her submission. She flung her arms around him, locking him against her.

His heart thundered in time to hers, and she never wanted to let go.

Because there, under a starry Texas sky, Olivia Faraday fell in love.

CHAPTER TEN

THE NEXT DAY it rained.

Not a pouring, cleansing rain, but a slobbery rain, drooling from a low gray sky. Olivia's newfound enthusiasm for the great outdoors was considerably dampened.

She and Luke had talked long into the night, sharing childhood memories. He'd grown up on a ranch—not this one, but another one in west Texas.

And Olivia had told him about her nomadic youth, following her parents and grandparents from acting job to acting job. She'd waited for him to ask where they were now, and when he had, she'd answered completely and honestly, not shielding the full extent of her financial responsibilities.

He hadn't flinched, not even when she carefully mentioned the amount the assisted-living home required for her grandparents' expenses, nor the subsidy she paid to her endearingly optimistic, but highly impractical parents. In fact, he'd nodded approvingly and told her how pleased he'd been to be able to help his own parents after disease had forced the destruction of their entire herd of cattle.

The fire had burned itself into orange embers about the same time the wind picked up and clouds covered the stars.

They'd parted after more soul-searing kisses, and Olivia had crawled into her tent, warmed by the glow of love.

As the front moved through, the wind buffeted the sides of her tent. Raindrops slapped the roof just inches from where she huddled in her sleeping bag. After a while, she could no longer ignore the sharp lumps on the ground or the cold seeping in. If only she could have slept, but instead, she'd listened to the rain and wind and thought. For hours.

She rehashed everything she and Luke had said to each other. For hours.

She explored her feelings about Luke. For hours.

Then she thought about her life as it was now and how Luke could be a part of it. For hours.

Eventually, even love's warm glow was no match for cold reality. And reality was that Luke loved this place and had no intention of giving any of it up. Reality was that Olivia, if she wanted a future with Luke, would be expected to give up her life in New York. Reality was that in doing so, she would bring with her a hefty financial obligation. Ranching was risky—look at his cash problems now. He did understand that her financial commitment would continue, didn't he?

On the other hand, nothing about a future had been said, had it? She'd been assuming a lot, hadn't she?

This back-and-forth fretting continued through the long, damp night.

Why couldn't she just have fallen asleep?

Before venturing out into the morning drizzle, Olivia poked her head through a bright orange plastic poncho with all the shape and allure of a garbage sack. She stowed her sleeping bag, hating to tie it onto Star in the rain. Tonight she'd sleep with the scent of wet horse.

The nylon tent was something else. It fit into a sausage-like case, or at least it did when it was dry. Olivia did her best, but water, leaves and bits of grass were rolled up with the tent.

Mud coated the knees of her jeans. Her stiff fingers could hardly work the rope.

This was the pits.

"How're you doing?" Luke approached with a mug of coffee and an intimate smile.

Olivia mustered a return smile. "Glad to see that coffee." She took a sip. Instant, yuck. At least it was hot. She tried to meet his eyes and couldn't.

A sour, charred smell hung in the air as the rain dripped on the blackened remains of last night's camp fire. Mother Nature had sent her a terrific metaphor.

"Maybe the rain will stop soon," Olivia wished aloud.

"Nah." Luke shook his head. "The front has stalled. The warm air from the Gulf meets the cool air from the Rockies, and we're in the middle. We're lucky." He smiled, delighted by the drizzly day. "We need the rain."

"I need a roaring fire and a snifter of brandy."

"Before breakfast?" He chuckled and slipped an arm around her waist, obviously attributing her mood to the weather. She'd allow him to think so. Besides, it could very well be the truth.

She and Luke trudged over to the van.

No breakfast.

The others, also garbed in ponchos and looking like a bunch of giant traffic pylons, stood and glared.

"Who was responsible for breakfast?" Luke demanded.

"Joel."

"And where is Joel?"

Silently they all looked toward the lone pup tent that was still standing. Luke strode across the fire circle and unzipped the front of the tent.

Olivia could hear him speaking, but not what he said.

"Man, it's raining out there!" Joel's protest cut through the campsite. "I ain't goin' nowhere."

Olivia waited for Luke to lower the boom, but as far as she could tell, he didn't say anything. He zipped up the tent with Joel inside and walked toward them.

Obviously Joel wouldn't be cooking this morning. Opening the back of the van, Olivia climbed in and surveyed their supplies. As was the custom, raw ingredients for a number of dishes were there. The cook decided the menu. Last night, she and Angel had fixed skillet corn bread with dinner and now Olivia searched for the leftovers.

Luke appeared in the doorway. "Breakfast was Joel's job."

"But Joel didn't do it." There was the corn bread, wrapped in aluminum foil.

"So the group will go without breakfast."

Olivia peeled away the foil. "Not if I can help it."

"You'll only teach the others that if they don't carry out their jobs, one of us will do them," he warned.

Reaching into the tiny cooler, Olivia removed an opened half-gallon carton of milk and thrust it at Luke. His arms automatically came up to hold it.

"Do you honestly think a hunk of cold corn bread is going to cause a mutiny?" She jumped from the van and began cutting modest-sized pieces, which she distributed to Angel and the boys.

"That's not the point," Luke muttered under his breath. "The point is that when someone lets the group down, the group suffers."

"Oh, I'm suffering all right." Olivia began pouring milk into paper cups. "I'm cold, wet and sore. I see no reason to be hungry, too." She offered him milk and corn bread. After staring from it to Joel's zipped tent, Luke accepted a piece.

The day went downhill from there.

They left camp without Joel, who emerged from his tent and stared at them in shocked disbelief as they trotted past.

Olivia had very mixed feelings about abandoning Joel. What if he couldn't find them? What if something happened to him? How would Luke explain it to Joel's parents?

Did Luke have a good personal-injury lawyer on retainer?

Every five minutes, Olivia twisted around in the saddle, searching for a flash of neon orange bobbing in the distance.

Worrying about Joel temporarily distracted her from her own discomfort. The rain spit on them all morning. Thinking Star must be uncomfortable, as well, Olivia spread her poncho to cover as much of the horse as possible. This trapped Star's body heat and warmed Olivia, but she occasionally caught the pungent whiff of sweaty horse.

Lunch was about as bad as breakfast. More bologna sandwiches. Olivia had hoped for a fire and maybe some soup, but supposed building a fire in the rain would be too difficult.

They were ready to mount and begin the afternoon stretch of their trek when Joel trotted up. A relieved

Olivia was ready to forgive all and welcome him back into the fold, but Luke barely nodded in acknowledgment and didn't offer the boy a sandwich.

Rafe pointed to Angel, leaned over and said something that brought an angry flush to Joel's face. "Leave me alone, man!"

Rafe laughed and maneuvered his horse next to Angel. "Want some company, chickie-mama?"

Not again. Olivia sighed and urged Star forward, positioning herself as chaperon for the rest of the afternoon.

By one o'clock she was ready to stop for the night.

By two o'clock she managed to convince Star to trot to the head of the line. "Can we set up camp early?" she asked Luke.

"Nope. Van won't know where to find us."

Olivia groaned.

Luke smiled and turned to her, began to say something and stopped, a startled expression on his face.

"What?" She watched his eyes flick upward to her hat. She touched the brim. "Oh, yeah. The feather is ruined, right?"

"Uh . . . yes." He turned back to the path.

Puzzled, Olivia felt her hat again. It was wet of course, and she supposed it wouldn't look like much when it dried, but Luke's hat was wet, and he didn't seem concerned. In fact, he'd pointed out that the curved brim funneled water away from the cowboy's shirt collar. But now that she thought about it, her brim wasn't turned up as much as she remembered.

She rode next to Luke for a few more minutes, hoping to absorb some of his contentment, but a familiar screech from the rear of the line of horses told her she needed to ride back there with Angel.

By three o'clock Olivia decided she'd had enough even though the drizzle had stopped. If they made camp now, Luke could ride to the rendezvous point with the van and direct it to them. She thought pitching camp before it rained again was a good idea, but he wouldn't listen.

By four o'clock Olivia vowed to hijack the van and bribe the driver to take her back to the ranch. The magic spell that had been cast on her by the fire last night had long since washed away. She was cold. Bone-deep cold. Her fingers were wrinkled. She smelled like a horse. Wet denim chafed her legs. Water had dripped into her boots.

By five o'clock her hat was definitely drooping. Olivia tried reshaping it, curling the limp brim over her fingers. Water from the sodden material dripped down the sides of her face. She brushed it away. Taking the reins again, she caught sight of her fingers. Her hands were so cold, they'd turned blue. No, make that greenish blue.

"Look at this," she said to Angel, and held out her hand. "I've been wet so long mold is growing." She laughed, surprised she still could.

Angel glanced from Olivia's hands to her face and quickly averted her gaze.

Just then, Luke mercifully called a halt. The van was nowhere in sight, but Olivia wasn't going to argue. She slipped down from Star before he could change his mind.

The sky was clearing, and Olivia decided to risk taking her poncho off. She removed her hat and propped it on the saddle horn.

Bedraggled peacock feathers fluttered limply. What was the matter with them? Is that what they did when they were still attached to the peacock? Didn't it ever rain on peacocks?

She shrugged off her poncho and grabbed her hat, smoothing out the feathers, encouraging the brim to curve—dyeing her hands green.

Olivia grimaced in disgust just as the supply van rumbled into the campsite. The others had gathered for their chore assignments and were giving Joel a hard time. Olivia sighed and rubbed her hands on her jeans. How could she stand three more days of this?

The supply van wasn't alone. Another, smaller van trailed behind it.

She saw Luke approach the driver of the supply van and gesture to the other vehicle. The driver shook his head and both men looked at her.

At that moment, the sliding door opened and a vision emerged. A vision clad in designer jeans, which hugged a figure that had subsisted on lettuce and mineral water for days. Not barbecue or corn bread or biscuits or gravy or... Olivia quit torturing herself.

The vision hopped to the ground and was followed by a photographer and Bettina Lynne.

Bettina Lynne? Olivia's mouth dropped open. What was the *Soap Bubbles* reporter doing out here? And who was that with her?

Abandoning Star, Olivia approached the newcomers. More people emerged from the van. Oh, swell. Bettina had brought a film crew.

Even though it was no longer raining, an assistant held an umbrella over Bettina and the other woman.

Olivia rolled her eyes. Bettina had gone Western, with boots, a suede skirt topped by a painted denim vest and enough turquoise to outfit an entire Indian tribe.

"*What* are you people doing out here?" Luke stalked over to Bettina, kicking aside cables.

Bettina gestured for her crew to continue setting up. "Taping a couple of quick promo spots. Don't mind us. Just go ahead with whatever you were doing." She shooed him away.

Luke wouldn't be shooed. Bettina was nuts to try.

"Oh, and tell Olivia we need her over here."

Olivia felt as though she'd stepped into a surreal foreign art film. Here was her world colliding with Luke's world. He stood there, defending his land, challenging the interlopers. They were in big trouble. This cowboy was tough. This cowboy looked like he could do some serious damage to persons, places and things.

Only nobody in the other world—the TV world—noticed. They set up lights and cameras. Called "Action."

Olivia turned her head and saw Star, chomping away on wet weeds. Angel and the boys were pitching their tents as if nothing had changed. Rafe and Joel were sniping at each other.

Then she looked at the camera crew, setting up as if they were in a TV studio.

It was so incredibly bizarre.

A watery sun leaked through the tattered clouds seconds before artificial light flooded Bettina and the other woman. Bettina brought the microphone to her chin and turned on a smile. "Bettina Lynne on location with a *Soap Bubbles* exclusive. Here with me—" she pulled the other woman into the frame "—is Andrea Craig who has just been cast as Megan Malloy on *Lovers and Liars*."

Megan Malloy. Diana D'Angelo's cousin. The other candidate for the coma. Olivia narrowed her gaze as she took in the full theatrical makeup, glossy raven tresses, snapping green eyes and expensive fringed suede. Olivia blinked. The actress looked like a young Diana D'Angelo! A fresh, sag-free, wrinkle-free Diana. A less-experienced-and-therefore-cheaper Diana.

A horrified fascination drew Olivia closer to the scene.

"Tell me," said Belinda, "is Megan going to cause some trouble for her cousin?"

"I guess so." Andrea hunched her shoulders and giggled. *Giggled.*

Bettina, pro that she was, smoothly inserted enough information so her viewers would know what was going on. "And Andrea will be joining fellow castmate Olivia Faraday as a volunteer at Bluebonnet Ranch."

"What?" Luke thundered.

"Cut." Bettina dropped the microphone. "Mr. Chance, *please,* I'm interviewing."

Luke didn't budge. "The only way she could help is by leaving."

"Which we will all do as soon as we finish taping," Bettina said pointedly.

He promptly stepped out of camera range and she resumed speaking. "For those of you who didn't see our interview with Olivia Faraday, *Lovers and Liars*, the once top-rated soap—" Olivia winced "—is gambling that the cowboy mystique will rein in the viewers. They've committed to an unheard of month-long shoot on location here at Bluebonnet Ranch. For over a week, Olivia Faraday has been out in the wilderness—" the camera panned the horizon "—*alone* with the handsome Lucas Chance, Bluebonnet's owner." Bettina leaned toward the camera in her trademark I'm-telling-a-secret pose. "Shall we find out if there's any truth to the rumors?"

Olivia wanted to strangle Bettina, but it seemed as if Luke might beat her to it.

"Well, Olivia?" Bettina turned to her side and found Andrea still standing there. The reporter dropped her microphone in frustration. "All right, cowboy, I told you to get Olivia Faraday, pronto!"

Luke took a menacing step forward, but Olivia was already on the move. "Over here, Bettina."

"Olivia!" Luke held out a hand. "Wait—"

"It'll just take a minute, Luke."

The camera swung toward her, and Olivia concentrated on slipping into her Diana mode, finding it surprisingly difficult. Smiling a wide Diana smile, she stepped into place opposite Andrea and only then registered Bettina's stunned expression.

Oblivious to the camera, Bettina was slack-jawed.

The hat. It did look awful. Casually, still smiling, Olivia slipped it from her head and shook her hair, running her fingers through it in the patented Diana gesture. Ugh, her hair felt horrible.

Bettina's eyes widened, and she covered her mouth and nose with her hand.

Okay. Her hair must look as horrible as it felt.

"She's not Olivia Faraday, is she?" asked Andrea, wrinkling her nose. "Gosh, what happened?"

Suddenly Olivia visualized how she must appear. She'd been on the trail for days. She wore no makeup. Her clothes were muddy and very likely smelly. "Listen, Bettina, let me freshen up a bit and then we'll continue the interview." She began backing away.

"We don't have that much time." Grinning, Bettina grabbed her arm. "This is *great.*" She brought the microphone into place, but broke up with laughter. "Are you still rolling?"

The cameraman indicated he was.

"Can you get a close-up?"

The crew was laughing now, and Andrea looked at Olivia as if she were a bug.

Something was wrong.

"Stop!" Luke strode in front of the camera, blocking the shot. "Olivia, get back."

Bettina's assistant came up behind Luke and shoved him out of the way.

"Keep filming!" Bettina screamed. Into her mike, she began to ad-lib. "Controversy is boiling on the set of *Lovers and Liars* as aging diva Diana D'Angelo bows to Father Time and the next generation. And what was actress Olivia Faraday's reaction when she met Andrea Craig, the hot new ingenue tapped to play Megan Malloy? One might say she was *green* with envy!" Bettina chortled.

Green with... Olivia stared at her hands, still holding her hat. She squeezed. Drops of green water formed and spread over her fingers, outlining the ridges. Glancing at Luke, she pointed a finger to her cheek.

He nodded with a grimace and touched his hair.

Her hair, too? She jammed the hat back on and turned away. Okay, so her face and hair were green. How could she salvage this?

"Andrea," she heard Bettina say. "You won the role of Megan due to your resemblance to Olivia Faraday—"

"Oh, I *hope* not!" Andrea broke in. "She looks awful!"

Bettina smiled maliciously, which told Olivia her picture and Andrea's stupid comment would be plastered on tabloids in every supermarket across the country before the week was out.

Something snapped inside her. She had nurtured the Diana image for years—her entire adult life. And now no one would ever see her in the same way again. She'd been every woman's fantasy.

Bettina was going to destroy that fantasy.

She was going to destroy Olivia's career, her security.

Olivia couldn't let that happen.

The camera. She had to get the videotape out of the camera.

That's all she thought of as she ran toward the cameraman, colliding with him and causing him to drop his equipment.

Unfortunately it was secured by a strap and didn't fall to the ground. Undeterred, Olivia wrestled it out of the man's grasp and punched buttons, hoping one would eject the tape.

"Stop her!" screamed Bettina.

The crew pulled at her, dragging her away from the camera. Luke fought to get to her side as she struggled to free her arms.

The cameraman regained control of the camera and focused it on her.

"Stop," she pleaded, tears of frustration pooling in her eyes. "Bettina, please."

"Let her go!" At Luke's sharp command, Bettina's assistant and the lighting technician released Olivia. She jerked her arms away and lunged at the camera, only to be held back once more.

Bettina moved in. "In a shocking development, *Soap Bubbles* was able to obtain exclusive footage of actress Olivia Faraday's nervous breakdown—"

"No!" Olivia shrieked.

"I *said* let her go!" Luke pulled the lighting technician away, and Olivia felt herself being lifted. An instant later, Luke enfolded her in his arms.

Olivia sagged against him, sobbing. "Everything's ruined!"

"Shh," he soothed, stroking her back. "I won't let anything—"

Suddenly the boys began shouting and pointing.

"Hey!" Gesturing wildly, Luke's supply-van driver tore across the clearing. The engine of the supply van rumbled into life. Tires spun and mud sprayed over everyone. Luke ducked, shielding Olivia. "What the—"

"My skirt!" Bettina screeched after the quickly disappearing van. "Look at the mud on my skirt!"

"Mr. Luke!" Angel ran up to them. "Joel and Rafe stole your van!"

CHAPTER ELEVEN

"HOW COULD THIS have happened?" Mr. Collingsworth was not pleased. Neither was Mrs. Collingsworth. Both paced back and forth across the polished wood floor of Luke's modest ranch house.

Olivia, hair wrapped in a towel, rubbed a lemon wedge over her face. There was still a green tinge, but she didn't know whether to attribute it to the dye or to the sick feeling in her stomach.

Luke, his jaw set, stood at the window, staring at the knot of reporters that lingered in the yard.

He'd barely spoken to her since Rafe and Joel had taken the van nearly forty-eight hours earlier. The van had been found, abandoned and out of gas. The boys were gone.

In the heat of the moment, everyone had forgotten about Bettina and her crew.

Big mistake. The missing boys made the late-night news.

Olivia hadn't thought it possible that Luke could become any angrier. He withdrew into a cold silence, his features resembling an ice sculpture. She wanted to comfort him—and be comforted by him. But when she'd reached out, he'd frozen her with a look that said, "This is all your fault."

And in a way it was. If she hadn't been so concerned with her image and what Bettina would show, Luke would have been supervising the boys, instead of her scuffle with the cameraman.

"You've got to find those boys!" Mr. Collingsworth said for the eighth time.

Olivia was counting. She wondered how many times Luke could swallow Mr. Collingsworth's increasingly barbed remarks without exploding. She was about to scream herself. A person could stand only so much guilt.

"And *this*." He gestured with one of an assortment of lurid tabloids he'd brought with him. "Diana throwing her tantrum right on the front page."

"Actually, that's the one where she's attacking the cameraman," Mrs. Collingsworth corrected in a disapproving voice.

"Well, the result is the same, isn't it? Scandal," moaned Mr. Collingsworth. "In the entire forty-five year history of Collingsworth Industries, we've never had a hint of wrongdoing, much less a full-fledged scandal."

"Then how fortunate you have this opportunity to share with me," Olivia said, unable to remain silent any longer. She didn't know about Luke, but her tolerance had expired two scandal lectures ago.

"Diana, dear," Mrs. Collingsworth took up the lecture, "scandal isn't something we desire."

"We're going to have it aplenty if we don't find those boys!" Mr. Collingsworth declared again. This made number nine.

Luke slammed his fist against the window ledge. "I was in the middle of the search when you radioed me to come here. And I'm riding back until I find them!"

He stormed out, nine apparently his limit.

Olivia wished she could leave, too. Another couple of soapings and the green should be gone from her hair. Fortunately the dye didn't show up as much as it would have if she'd been a blonde, but as long as green tinged her forehead, she figured dye remained in her hair.

Besides, it was a good excuse for a bubble bath.

Bubble baths reminded her—and would forever after remind her—of Luke. How ironic that this disaster should occur just hours after she'd unlocked her heart.

Mr. Collingsworth cleared his throat. "Diana, in light of recent events, Mrs. C. and I must rethink our patronage of your program."

Olivia had wondered when they'd get around to that. She knew her contract was up for renewal. Mr. Collingsworth undoubtedly knew it, too. But what he might not realize was if he insisted on getting rid of Diana, John Paul wouldn't set foot back on Bluebonnet Ranch. There would be no need. Luke wouldn't get his money. Even if—and it was a big if—*Lovers and Liars* found a new sponsor who insisted on continuing the ranch story line, it'd be too late to help Luke. He'd lose the ranch.

"Without your sponsorship, *Lovers and Liars* probably won't continue the ranch story line." Olivia gazed steadily at Mr. Collingsworth. Luke might hate her now, but she couldn't hate him and she wouldn't be the cause of his losing the ranch he loved.

"But everyone knows Diana will inherit the ranch," Mrs. C. protested. "They've already talked about it on the show."

Shrugging, Olivia set the lemon wedge on a saucer in front of her. "When Diana comes back, she'll just announce that she sold it. Story lines disappear all the time." Too bad the Collingsworths didn't know they were witnessing an Emmy-caliber, it-makes-no-difference-to-me act.

Distressed, Mrs. Collingsworth tugged at her husband's coat as he paced near her. "But Luke—"

"I don't know." Shaking his head, Mr. Collingsworth examined the tabloids. Olivia didn't tell him that there would likely be different pictures in the tabloids that were published later in the week. Bettina certainly had plenty of material to peddle.

"If the reporters hadn't been there, those boys wouldn't have run off. And if we can't find them all safe and sound, then we'll have *that* to weather." He sighed. "Two scandals at once. Collingsworth Industry stock would nose-dive."

Olivia grabbed the lemon wedge and rubbed it on her hands and face again. Mr. Collingsworth was far more concerned with the effect scandal would have on his precious business than he was with the safety of the boys.

The phone rang in Luke's office, as it had steadily since their return. Moments later, Angel appeared in the doorway. "For you, Olivia." Great. Either her agent screaming or John Paul screaming. "It's your mother."

"My *mother?*" How much worse could it get?

Angel nodded. "I need a break. I'll be in the stables," she said in an undertone, and left through the kitchen.

"You see?" Olivia heard Mrs. Collingsworth say. "Diana talks to her mother. We *ought* to give her another chance."

Olivia shook her head as she shut the door to Luke's office. "Mom?" She tried to sound happy. She didn't want her mother worrying about Olivia's job.

"Congratulations, Livvie! Your father and I are so proud of you!"

Two heartbeats went by. "Have you read any papers recently?"

"Of course. That's why we called."

"Mom...I'm okay. The pictures make everything seem worse." The photograph of her face had obviously been retouched. The allover green made her look like the Wicked Witch of the West.

"Oh, they always do," was her mother's cheerful response. "Isn't it great?"

"No!" Olivia howled, for once unamused by her mother's zany interpretation of things. "I look awful!"

"I know! The stores will probably sell out. Your father had to go to three different supermarkets this morning to buy extra copies. You will autograph them for us, won't you?"

"Mother..." Olivia closed her eyes and let out a long sigh.

"Your grandparents send their love."

Olivia winced. "Some people might consider this bad publicity."

"The only bad publicity is no publicity. This will be great for your career."

"How?" She couldn't wait to hear.

"Because this is mainstream press." In spite of herself, Olivia smiled at the thought of tabloids being considered mainstream press.

"They wouldn't bother to print anything about you if you weren't somebody important," her mother continued.

Olivia straightened and opened her eyes. It máde sense in a weird way.

"You're going to attract a lot of attention. I just know something big will come of this, Livvie. Be alert for ways to use the publicity to your advantage."

Olivia sat in the relative peace of Luke's office for several minutes after her conversation with her mother. She hated it when her mother made sense. It always caused Olivia to wonder if she was the one going crazy.

The phone rang—surprise, surprise—and she answered it.

"Olivia, dear, is that you?" John Paul. That *was* a surprise. Her stomach tightened. Here it was. The sack.

"Get back to New York as fast as you can. The overnight ratings have skyrocketed. The viewers want you, darling, and we've got to film something to show them. Hurry, and we can do a head shot of you talking on the telephone and splice it into Friday's show."

"What?" This was the last thing she expected.

But John Paul hadn't stopped talking. "We already inserted some of that ranch footage we shot in today's and tomorrow's shows. You're hot, hot, hot."

"But—" Olivia took a deep breath "—I have to tell you the Collingsworths are in the next room, and they might pull out as sponsors."

"Let 'em," John Paul said promptly. "The ratings are up. Advertisers are standing in line."

"John Paul, the photos have only been out since yesterday." Much as she wanted to believe him, John Paul's hype was legendary.

"But your film clips made the national news!" He chortled in delight.

"Mine?"

"Yes, dear. You looked quite ferocious."

The national news. Olivia wanted to shrivel. Melt. Evaporate. Any hope she had of groveling to the Collingsworths had just disappeared.

"You can't *buy* publicity like this!" The producer gloated.

"Who'd want to?"

"It's *wonderful!*" John Paul gushed. Olivia held the receiver away from her ear. "We're going to be back on top!"

There was a commotion in the living room. Olivia cracked open the office door, wondering if the Collingsworths had come to blows.

Luke was back.

"John Paul, I've got to go—"

"Pack! Yes! Hurry!"

She ran into the other room just in time to catch a grim Luke holding the door open for the Collingsworths.

"Luke?"

At the sound of her voice, Mrs. Collingsworth turned a tearful face toward her. "I'm sorry, Diana. But it's for your own good. I'm sending you the name of a good therapist." Her husband tugged her away. "Goodbye!"

"What happened?" Olivia asked as Luke shut the door behind them. "Did you find the boys?"

"Yes and no." He ran his fingers through his hair, a look of utter weariness on his face. "They wandered into the branding crew's camp. Simon's picking them up now."

Olivia sank onto the sofa. "What a relief."

"Yes." Luke joined her, leaned back and stared at the ceiling. "Joel and Rafe are members of different gangs back in the city. They wanted to have it out, one on one." Luke rubbed his forehead and sighed. "They left the trail, got lost and drove around in circles all night until they ran out of gas." He gave a short, mirthless laugh. "Neither one really knows how to drive."

They could have killed themselves. Olivia knew Luke had thought the same thing.

"Are the boys okay?"

"Funny thing," Luke said, propping his booted feet on the coffee table. They were caked with mud. "Those kids discovered they had to depend on each other. Which was what I was trying to teach them in the first place." Luke closed his eyes. "All's well that ends well."

But had it ended well?

Olivia pulled the towel off her head and dropped it over the tabloids Mrs. Collingsworth had left on the coffee table. No use rubbing salt into the wounds.

The silence stretched, but at least he hadn't thrown her out. "What happened with the Collingsworths?"

"Bad news. They're gone."

"That's not bad news."

Luke turned his head to look at her. "Olivia... they're not going to sponsor your show anymore."

"I figured as much. They were worried that being associated with me would cause their stock to nose-dive." Olivia laughed lightly. "Isn't that ridiculous?" She waited for Luke to agree with her. "I said, isn't that ridiculous?"

Finally Luke shrugged. "They're very conservative. They're not going to contribute to the Bluebonnet Foundation anymore, either."

"Oh, Luke." No wonder he looked so defeated. "I...I'm sorry." How inadequate. He probably blamed her for everything.

"Doesn't matter. Once I heard they'd pulled out of your show, I knew the Bluebonnet program was down the tubes."

"I'll talk to them...."

His mouth curved upward a fraction. "I don't think you have a whole lot of influence with them right now."

Olivia suddenly sat up. "Then we'll find more contributors. You'll still have the Bluebonnet Ball, won't you?"

Luke shook his head. "You don't understand. The foundation is solvent. The ranch isn't. I'm not going to be able to hang on to it. There'd be no place for the kids to come."

"But—"

"Don't beat yourself up over it." He reached out and caressed her cheek with his finger. "Collingsworth was getting on my nerves, anyway."

"Luke." Olivia captured his hand. "You're not going to lose the ranch."

His smile all but patted her on the head. "I may be a simple cowpoke," he said in an exaggerated drawl, "but I know y'all were only filming here to indulge the Collingsworths."

"Right, but—"

"Your producer didn't much like it here, and he's not about to come back if he doesn't have to. And if he doesn't come back, I'm not getting any money."

"Luke—"

"No money, no ran—"

Olivia kissed him. Honestly, it was the only way.

Luke instantly abandoned talking for kissing. His hand tangled in her wet hair as he kissed her with raw hunger.

Olivia's momentum carried her forward until Luke fell full-length onto the couch, his arm keeping her sprawled on top of him.

"*Something* good came out of this, at least," he murmured, pulling her head down.

"Luke," she gasped, coming up for air. "You're not going to lose the ranch, because we're still filming here."

He nuzzled the side of her neck. "I figure you're feeling sorry for me, but I'll take it."

"Really." She had to make him understand. "The ranch story stays. I'm 'hot, hot, hot.'"

Luke grinned and settled her firmly against him. "I know, know, know."

IT TOOK AWHILE—a long while—but Olivia was able to convince Luke that *Lovers and Liars* was going to film on his ranch as scheduled. His relief, deep and uncensored, showed her that he was capable of Emmy-winning, I-don't-care performances, too.

There was much more to be said, but Simon drove into the ranch yard with the boys, and within the hour, Olivia and Angel were on their way to the Austin airport.

A limousine waited for Olivia in New York. The driver handed her a script and a frantic message from John Paul demanding she come to the studio immediately. He was prepared to tape all night if necessary and requested that she learn her lines on the drive over.

When Olivia saw Angel's wide eyes, she invited her along.

"This is it?" Angel asked as she stepped into Olivia's tiny dressing room. "I thought you were a big star."

Olivia shoved a pile of mail off a chair and gestured for Angel to sit. "I am a big star. I don't have to share." She flipped on the lights around her mirror.

Angel didn't look convinced. She started to straighten the stacks of letters, old scripts, coffee mugs and bits and pieces of wardrobe. "So many letters. When do you have time to read them all?"

"I don't." Olivia glanced up from the script. "I cart them over to my publicist who screens them. A lot are requests for appearances or photographs. She'll respond to the letters she can, but I read all the personal ones and try to answer—"

Angel gasped. "There are boxes full of letters back here!"

"And several more in my office," said John Paul from the doorway. He eyed Angel suspiciously. "Are you armed?"

Angel looked right at him. "Yes."

John Paul stayed in the doorway. "Olivia, your hair is dreadful. Let's pull it back and put a cowboy hat on you. Wardrobe!" he shouted, moving down the hall.

"Do you pay the publicist?" Angel asked as Olivia began applying makeup.

"Boy, do I," Olivia answered. "But this is an unusual amount of mail. I was on vacation right before we went to Bluebonnet and then with the little incident on the wilderness trip..." She trailed off, not wanting to rehash all that.

Angel didn't comment, but continued straightening the dressing room. When Olivia finished her makeup, she said, "It sounds a lot more exciting than it is, but would you like to watch the taping? If you get bored, you can come back here."

When they reached the set, Olivia was surprised to see Andrea there.

The ingenue regarded her warily, and Olivia knew she'd have to make the first move.

"I want to apologize for the other day," she said, though she was not at all sorry.

"Oh, that's okay," Andrea said breezily. "I've heard that hormones can really act up in a woman your age."

Olivia maintained her smile just a moment longer. She and Andrea were not going to bond. Ever.

It was nearly four in the morning when they finished. Olivia had forgotten all about Angel. But when she pushed open her dressing-room door, there was Angel, asleep on the love seat. And Olivia's dressing room was immaculate.

"Angel," she said, nudging the girl's shoulder. "You didn't have to do this, but I'm awfully glad you did."

Angel stretched, sat up and blinked. "I sorted your mail, too." She pointed to the three boxes by the door. "That box is picture requests, the middle one is where I put the letters that ask you stuff, and that third box is all the letters I didn't know what to do with. Oh, and I threw away the marriage proposals and smutty letters from weirdos." She made a face. "There are some strange people out there."

"You're a doll. Thanks." Olivia tossed her cowboy hat onto the dressing table. Now there was room.

"You need a personal assistant," Angel announced. "And I want the job."

Olivia opened her mouth to say no, but "personal assistant" did have a nice ring to it. "What about school?" she asked, instead.

"I'll come after school."

Angel looked so determined and so eager. It would make Olivia's life much easier... "You've got yourself a job."

"OLIVIA, BABE, I'm telling you, you're in! They want you, babe. Only you."

Her agent was panting. "Calm down." Olivia glanced over her shoulder at Angel, sitting cross-legged on the floor of Olivia's dressing room. Angel had been her personal assistant for five days, and Olivia wondered how she'd ever gotten along without her. The rest of the cast eyed Angel covetously. If Olivia didn't watch it, they'd steal her. "Run the details by me again, Tony?"

It was a fantasy. A dream come true. A glitzy prime-time television series centering on three high-powered women executives. The network wanted fresh but experienced actresses, and Olivia Faraday fit the bill. The part sounded a lot like Diana, but it meant that Olivia could finally make the break to nighttime television.

Olivia's hands were shaking as she clung to the telephone. Her mother had been right. Apparently any publicity was better than no publicity.

The money would be great if the show was picked up. Right now, the network had committed to a pilot and six episodes. Olivia could hardly stand it. If the show had a long run, she and her family would be set for life.

"So when would we start shooting the pilot?"

"Two weeks."

"But I've got another month left on my *Lovers and Liars* contract."

"Don't worry—we'll work it out. You can double up the taping if you have to. It's been done before."

"But... we're scheduled to film Diana's ranch story next month." And if she didn't film the ranch story—

"*Olivia!* Babe, Diana's kaput. You're outta there. This is *it*. The big time. You can't do both."

"What if *Boardroom Belles* doesn't make it? Or it's canceled? Then I'll be out of a job."

She could almost hear Tony shrug. "You gotta take that chance."

Could she? Should she?

And what would happen to Luke? The ranch?

"I'll think about it, Tony."

"*Think?* What's there to think about?"

Luke. The ranch. Her family. Her future. Everything. "It's a big decision. I need time."

She could hear Tony's breath hiss between his teeth. "I'll try to stall them. Just remember, you may be hot now, but you'll cool quickly."

"TAG, YOU'RE IT," said Luke's exasperated voice on Olivia's answering machine. "Call me back in the middle of the night if you have to, but I want to talk to *you*, not this machine!"

Olivia knew how he felt because she felt the same way. They'd played telephone tag for days. She glanced at her watch as she punched his number. It was midafternoon, and she had a break while other scenes were being filmed. A break she was going to use to think about her agent's call.

She needed to talk to Luke now more than ever.

Luke's answering machine picked the phone up on the fourth ring, and Olivia hung up in frustration.

She rewound the latest message and played it again, just to hear his voice. In the middle of the third repetition, her apartment intercom buzzed.

"Olivia?"

"*Luke?*" It couldn't be.

But it was. Minutes later, Olivia opened the door to a big bouquet of yellow roses.

"I wanted to remind you of Texas," Luke explained as he took her in his arms.

"I didn't know until this very moment that yellow roses were my favorite," she said, tilting her face to meet his lips.

For just a moment Olivia lost herself in Luke's kiss.

For just a moment.

"We have to talk." They spoke at the same time.

Laughing, Olivia led the way to her kitchen, dumping out an artificial arrangement of flowers to use the vase for her roses. "Look at you." She nodded at his suit in appreciation. He looked as great in the Armani as he did in his jeans. "What are you doing in New York?"

"Business with the foundation, but that was really an excuse to come and see you." Luke stood behind her, arms wrapped around her waist. "To see if you missed me as much as I missed you." There was a hint of a question in his voice.

Olivia dropped the roses on the counter and turned in his arms. "Oh, yes!" She hugged him tightly.

"You know, it's the darnedest thing." His voice rumbled against her ear. "I thought I had a full life, but once you were gone, it seemed empty."

Olivia blinked rapidly. "I know." Her voice was strangled.

He pulled back to see her. "What are we going to do about it?"

"I...I don't know..." What was she going to do? How could she tell him?

He led her to the chintz sofa and faced her, holding her hands, his knees touching hers.

Oh, no. He was going to propose.

Olivia couldn't breathe. Her heart started pounding so hard she could hear it and only it. She could see Luke's lips move, but she couldn't hear the words he spoke. All she could hear was the panicked thudding in her ears.

She stared at his lips, trying to make out what he was saying. The ranch. He was talking about the ranch. Olivia's heart slowed enough for her to hear.

"I wanted you to know about the plans I've got." He gazed at her steadily, and Olivia understood that he was outlining the kind of life he wanted. The kind of life she'd have if she chose to share it with him.

As he talked about his dreams, she watched his face and realized the ranch was his true love, whether or not he realized it. He might be wearing the uniform of a successful city dweller, but his heart—his soul—was back in Texas.

And Olivia knew she loved him. But Luke without the ranch wouldn't be Luke.

Where did she fit in? Someone had to ask first.

She squeezed his hands. "What about me?" Taking a deep breath, she asked, "Do I fit in anywhere?"

"Do you want to?" he asked quietly.

Her eyes stung and she looked down at their clasped hands. "Say I—if I—lived on the ranch all the time, what would I do?"

"Do?" He laughed. "There's always plenty to do. You should have learned that."

Swallowing, she asked, "You mean like mucking out the stables, cleaning, cooking, chaperoning girls, maybe a little bookkeeping?"

"And loving and laughing—and making babies."

Now she faced him squarely. "But not acting."

"I know it's important to you." He met her gaze. "I don't want a weekend wife. I want someone as committed to me as I am to her."

Olivia freed her hands, and got up and walked into her bedroom. She withdrew a file from her desk and returned to lay it open on the coffee table. "This is how much money I made last year." She handed him her tax forms. His eyes widened. "And to refresh your memory, this is how much I spent on my parents and grandparents."

"We could swing it without your income if we had to." He carefully inserted the paper into the file. "Or they could live at the ranch."

Olivia said nothing. Her grandparents loved where they lived. Several other aging actors from vaudeville days resided there, as well, which was one reason Olivia and her parents had selected the home.

Luke stood and held out his hand to her. "It's a lot to think about," he said, pulling her close. "But we could make it work."

Long after Luke left, Olivia sat in her darkening apartment. He hadn't come right out and asked her to give up everything for him—and he wouldn't. It had to be her choice.

The horrible thing was, if Olivia accepted the *Boardroom Belles* role, Luke would lose the ranch and there would be no choice to make.

She would never love the ranch the way Luke did. And he would never be happy in New York—or Los Angeles, which is where she'd have to move if she did *Boardroom Belles*. Love might carry them through for a while, but they were both mature enough to realize that resentment would creep in and sour their relationship.

He thought he was giving her time, thought he'd see her again when *Lovers and Liars* arrived to tape.

A mauve glow pinkened the sky before Olivia made her decision—the only one she really could.

Before she changed her mind, she picked up the phone to call her agent.

And refuse the offer.

CHAPTER TWELVE

"DIANA IS DEAD."

"I can see that." Olivia threw the script on John Paul's desk. "What I want to know is why."

John Paul leaned back in his chair and steepled his fingers. "Don't play dumb with me, Olivia. After working together for thirteen years, you might have told me you were thinking of leaving the show. At least you could've given me the opportunity to warn the writers to plan for a graceful exit. Or perhaps an exit not quite so final."

"I wasn't planning an exit."

He dropped his hands and stood. "The secret is out, my dear. I know all about the part you were offered on *Boardroom Belles.*"

"You obviously don't know that I turned it down."

"Ha!" John Paul showed his theatrical roots. "No actress in her right mind would turn down a juicy plum like that."

"*I* did."

"If that's true, then you're a fool."

Or in love, she thought.

John Paul crossed his arms and walked around her, his gaze insolent. "Give it up, dear. I'm going to hold you to every minute left on your contract. We're milking Diana's death for all it's worth. The publicity will be tremendous. We expect ratings to go through the roof."

"I refused the part!" How did he find out about it, anyway?

"Better tell your agent, dear." He sauntered toward the door. "Oh, and if this was a gamble to increase the terms of your contract, you lost."

He left Olivia standing there, stunned.

What happened? Almost before the thought fully formed, she was on the phone to her agent.

"Changed your mind, didn't you?" Tony asked as soon as she was put through to him.

"No, I didn't. What did you tell the *Lovers and Liars* people?"

"I... They wanted to nail down the contract terms before they budgeted the Diana story line. I had to tell them about the *Boardroom Belles* offer."

Olivia closed her eyes. "You didn't tell them I accepted, did you?"

"I told them you were thinking about it. Babe, it was your big break."

Disaster. Olivia collapsed onto one of John Paul's chairs.

"Look, I've got a call into your producer—"

"Don't bother." Olivia rubbed her temples. "*Lovers and Liars* won't renew my contract. John Paul just killed Diana."

Silence. Then, "How?"

"She gets kicked in the head by a horse and falls into a coma from which she will not recover." Olivia had memorized the memo attached to the revised script.

"Can you talk them into amnesia? You know, Diana wanders off after getting kicked in the head? That way there's no body."

"I doubt it. John Paul is bent on extended hospital scenes and gruesome makeup."

"Ooh, an on-screen death. Real hard to bring back a character when the audience has seen the flat line. But hey, it's been done." Tony was ever the optimist. "Remember the *Bionic Woman*? They not only revived her, they gave her a whole new series!"

"Well, call the *Boardroom Belles* people and accept."

"Olivia...babe..."

Olivia began to shake. "You already called them, didn't you?" She wasn't going to have *any* job.

"Had to. They needed an answer."

"Call them back."

"Babe, I don't know... We might have better luck trying for amnesia or a continuing role as Diana's ghost. Or, I know! Her twin—"

"Call them."

Two days later, the cast of *Boardroom Belles* was announced. Olivia Faraday's name was not mentioned.

THE BLUEBONNETS were nearly gone, burned away in the late May sunshine. But Bluebonnet Ranch looked fresh and new.

The outside of the buildings sported a fresh coat of paint and the huge spray of bluebonnets remained on the bunkhouse. Inside the bunkhouse all the beds had new mattresses and the bathroom had been redone. The dirt road had been landscaped and fresh gravel lined the ranch yard.

And Diana D'Angelo was about to get kicked in the head by a horse.

Olivia, who had been on the set since six that morning, rested in the shade of her trailer, fanning herself with a white hat—she was taking no chances. The stunt team was blocking the accident, which was really no accident but an evil plot perpetrated by one Megan Malloy. Megan would then inherit the ranch that should've been hers in the first place, as well as take over the void left by Diana's demise.

The reporters, issued invitations by John Paul, flocked to the scene to film the end of one of the most popular and notorious characters in daytime television. Diana D'Angelo would go out on top.

Luke was with the stunt team, at first making sure they weren't abusing his horses, then watching in appreciation of their skill.

Olivia hadn't told him exactly what was going on and hoped he never figured out the significance of the scene they were about to tape.

"Olivia, how about a last interview for old time's sake?" Bettina Lynne thrust a microphone at her.

Olivia hesitated, but couldn't afford to alienate Bettina, even though Bettina had alienated *her.* She indicated she'd answer questions.

"Daytime viewers were stunned by the decision to kill off Diana. Did it come as a surprise to you?"

Yes, but she wasn't going to share that with Bettina. "I'm very fond of Diana. We grew up together. It'll be like losing a friend." Not to mention a paycheck.

"What are your plans after you leave the show?"

Olivia smiled. "Nothing that I'm prepared to discuss at this time." Standard interview talk covering everything from "the contract hasn't been signed" to "I haven't the foggiest idea."

"Rumor has it you were considered for a move to prime time. Is that true?"

Rats. Olivia started to run her fingers through her hair in the classic Diana gesture, then stopped. She wasn't going to be Diana anymore.

For the first time, it really sank in.

"I'd love to move to prime time," she said, responding without answering.

"Really?" Bettina drew out the word and smirked at the camera. "I heard you turned down a part on *Boardroom Belles*. Could Lucas Chance have anything to do with that?"

"Luke and I are just friends." Olivia automatically made the standard response as a movement behind Bettina caught her eye.

Luke stood there, hands clenched at his sides. He'd obviously overheard the interview.

"I thought we were more than friends," he said the moment Bettina left.

Maybe he hadn't heard about Diana. Olivia slipped her arm around his waist. "We are, but I wasn't going to tell Bettina." She smiled up at him.

He didn't smile back. In fact, he held his body stiffly away from her.

Olivia let her arms fall to her sides. "What's wrong?" she asked, afraid she already knew.

He hooked a thumb over his shoulder. "The stunt crew told me your character is being killed off. Why didn't you tell me?"

Somehow she wasn't surprised he'd found out. "I've only known a few days, myself."

"Days?"

Olivia looked down at her boots, the same ones she'd worn on the camping trip. This was the moment she'd been dreading.

Luke took her elbow. "C'mon." He firmly steered her toward the ranch house.

"Luke..." She didn't want to have this conversation. "I'm going to miss the accident!"

"Watch it on TV."

They were far from the action before he spoke again. "I can't figure you out. Getting killed off is a big deal, isn't it?"

Olivia gave a short laugh. "Yeah."

"And you never told me." He shook his head. "What about that question the reporter asked you? *Were* you offered a big part?"

"Yes." She closed her eyes briefly.

"How big?"

Olivia gestured to the ranch house. "Can we go in?"

Once inside, Olivia sank onto the couch and leaned back, propping her feet on the coffee table. As she stared at the ceiling, she remembered Luke's adopting an identical position the last time they were together in the ranch house.

This time, he sat next to her, leaning forward, his elbows on his knees. "Lady, back in New York, I spilled my guts to you. Did you ever care *anything* for me—or was that just another role you played?"

Olivia flinched at the bitterness in his voice. "Of course I cared. I—" She was about to tell him she loved him, but he slashed through her words.

"*Caring* means sharing." He grimaced. "I sound like a blasted greeting card." He got to his feet and prowled around the room.

In his office the telephone rang. He ignored it. "Why didn't you tell me any of this?"

"Because I turned down the part!" Olivia snapped.

"You turned down an opportunity like that?"

She nodded.

"At the very least, I would have expected you to mention it in passing." He turned to the window and stared out. "Apparently I overestimated the depth of your feelings."

How unfair. "I turned it down because of you!" Olivia flung at him all the words she'd been holding back.

"Without discussing it with me?" He gazed at her, aghast. "Why?"

"Because if I'd taken the *Boardroom Belles* part, I'd be in Los Angeles right now." She waited for the ramifications to sink in.

"So? Los Angeles, New York, what's the difference?"

Was she going to have to spell it out for him?

Luke paced back and forth in front of the window. "You're all supposed to be finished here by mid-month. I would've had a couple of days before the first group—" He stopped, a startled expression on his face.

Olivia held her breath.

Luke slowly turned toward her. "Only there wouldn't have been any filming here without Diana, is that it?"

Olivia nodded. Now he'd understand how much she loved him. She waited. Waited for an "Olivia, my love, I've misjudged you!" or maybe, "Olivia, darling, how can I ever thank you?" Then she'd get to show him how.

She was not prepared for the man in front of her to explode in fury. "How could you do something so asinine?"

What? "Don't you understand? You wouldn't have been paid! You would've lost the ranch!"

"Maybe. Maybe not. But you had no right to make the decision all on your own."

"Excuse me?" This conversation wasn't going anything like she expected. "I just saved your ranch for you."

"By passing up your big break! I wouldn't have asked that of you."

Olivia felt as if she'd been hit in the stomach. Apparently *she* was the one who'd misjudged their relationship. "Then what was all that talk about not wanting a weekend wife? All the never-ending chores, chaperoning camping trips." Olivia leapt to her feet. "And it can't have escaped your notice that I'm *not* camper material."

"The entire world knows you're not camper material," Luke said dryly.

"Well, how did you expect me to do everything?" She flung her arms out in a wide gesture. "Hop a flight during scene breaks?"

"If I recall that conversation correctly, you asked what there was to do here. I told you."

"But... *I can't live like that.*" There. It was out.

"I know." His mouth twisted in a wry smile. "I don't recall asking you to."

"Oh." Her legs collapsed and she sat on the couch in a poof. How humiliating. "I thought..."

"And you quit your soap part, too?"

"I didn't quit. They're not renewing my contract."

He raised an eyebrow, obviously waiting for more.

"John Paul found out about the series offer and assumed I'd accepted it," she explained. "He was mad because I hadn't told him in advance so he'd have time to adjust the story line."

"But you're a big deal on that show." He nodded at the video recorder. "I've been taping it."

"You've been watching *Lovers and Liars*?" Olivia was charmed by his admission.

"I fast-forward through everything but your scenes. So how come they're killing off Diana if you're still available?"

"Publicity and ratings. When John Paul thought I wasn't signing a new contract, he wanted to get the most out of the old one."

Luke's face softened. "So you sacrificed more than you expected to, is that it?"

"Yes," she said pointedly. She had as yet to hear any expressions of gratitude.

"What will you do now?"

She'd hoped a proposal of marriage was forthcoming. Since it apparently wasn't, couldn't he at least invite her to stay for a while? "I don't know," she admitted. "I kept hoping John Paul would change his mind."

The telephone rang again. Instead of answering it, Luke meandered over to the couch, obviously mulling over what she'd said. He raised his hands to his hips, staring down at her. "Let me see if I understand this correctly. A life on the ranch fills you with dread."

"I could learn to..." At Luke's searching look, Olivia nodded glumly, but he didn't seem offended.

"Your heart's desire is to make the jump to prime time," he continued, "but meanwhile, you're on top in daytime television."

"I was." Olivia nodded again.

"So you're offered the opportunity to star in a new television series. If you accept, you accomplish your dream *and—*" he raised a finger in the air "—as a bonus get rid of the ranch problem. How am I doing?"

She exhaled in a whoosh, blowing a lock of hair off her forehead. "That's about it."

"But what do you do with this perfect opportunity? You *refuse* the part to save the ranch and manage to lose your current role in the bargain."

Wincing, she crossed her arms over her chest. Boy, had she botched everything.

"Sounds like you'll have to audition for the role of ranch wife."

Maybe life on the ranch wouldn't be so bad. After all, there'd be some pretty incredible fringe benefits. She darted a glance at him and was surprised to see a look of tenderness in his eyes. "I was kind of hoping I'd get the part on past experience."

"Olivia..." Shaking his head, he sat next to her on the couch. "I don't know what to say."

"You could say, 'Thank you' or, 'I love you,' or something." Her voice clogged.

His blue eyes warmed, and he grinned crookedly. "Or something."

"What is this, a game of who'll-say-it-first?" she demanded.

"I love you." He leaned forward and just before he kissed her, he whispered, "I win."

"I like this game," Olivia murmured against his mouth.

After a moment Luke drew back. "You've got the part."

"Of ranch wife?" She snuggled next to him, resolutely thinking only of the joy of being with him and not the circumstances of their togetherness. She loved him and he'd be happy. She should quit complaining.

"Olivia, why did you try to help me keep the ranch?"

"Because I love you," she responded at once.

"And?" he prompted.

Wasn't that enough? Olivia sat up so she could see his face. "This ranch is part of you. Remember the night by the camp fire?" She smiled softly. "That's the night I fell in love with you. It's also the night I realized you'd never be happy living in the city. You wouldn't even be the same Luke in the city."

"You're right. And if I'd had to sell this place, I would've worked my tail off until I could buy another."

She shrugged. "So, here we are."

He pulled her close. "Olivia, much as I admire your willingness to be a ranch wife, if it's all the same to you, I'll take the wife part and we'll negotiate the rest."

"What do you mean?"

"It means I want to be married to you, but I know you'd be as unhappy here as I'd be in the city." He stroked her hair as she went weak with relief. "We'll have to work out the details."

"How?"

"I don't know yet. It'll take us a while and we might not get it right the first time, but won't it be fun to try?"

"Oh, Luke..." Olivia's heart was full. "I won't promise to love the ranch as much as I love you, but I can learn to appreciate it."

"And I can stand a couple more trips to the city each year." He bent his head. "You'll have to show me those lights you're so crazy about."

As she tilted her lips to meet his, the telephone rang again. Irritation crossed Luke's face. "Let's go unplug that thing."

They reached the office in time to hear Olivia's agent gasping as he tried to leave a message.

She picked up the phone. "Tony?"

"O-Olivia." Gasp, pant.

"I'm here."

"You—" gasp "—won't believe this!"

"Somebody backed out of *Boardroom Belles*?" she guessed, clutching at Luke's arm and holding the phone so he could hear.

"Better!"

"Calm down, Tony. You're hyperventilating."

"A movie."

She grinned at Luke and gave him a thumbs-up. "A TV movie? Tell me about it."

"No," Tony gasped. "A *movie* movie."

Olivia opened her mouth, but nothing came out.

Her agent took another breath, his voice quivering. "You knew something, didn't you? That's why you turned down *Boardroom Belles*."

"I—"

"What a player!" Tony managed to control his breathing long enough to tell her that she—and only she—had been invited to audition for a small but pivotal part in a motion picture. "They want your madwoman thing."

"Oh, great."

"Babe, it's a *movie!*"

She raised her eyebrows at Luke.

"Go for it," he mouthed.

Olivia grinned. "Make the arrangements, Tony, and see what else is out there. I'm ready to try for the big time."

"You got it, babe. But it might be awhile before something else comes up. This won't be the steady work you've been used to," he warned.

"Sounds perfect." The answer to everything.

"You sure?" her agent asked. "You might have to cool your heels for a few months."

With a radiant smile, Olivia gazed into Luke's eyes. "That'll be just the right amount of time for a Texas honeymoon."